The Fact Book of Show Jumping

By Tiina Vainikainen

The Fact Book of Show Jumping
© Tiina Vainikainen /Stabenfeldt A/S
The Author asserts her moral right to be identified as the Author of the
work in relation to all such rights as are granted by the Author to the
Publisher under the terms and conditions of the Agreement.
Original title: Estekirja
Cover layout: Stabenfeldt A/S
© Photos: Johanna Viitanen
© Photos of Piia Pantsu and Franke Sloothaak: Jan Gyllensten. Photo of
Maria Gretzer: Bettan Ryderheim.
© Photo page 38: Marielle Andersson Gueye
© Front cover photo: Bob Langrish.
Back cover photo: Jaakko Jauhiainen.
Text chapter 6, Hints and tips by famous riders: Pernilla Linder Velander.
© Illustrations: Jeanette Laine
© Illustrations on page 93 and 99: Charlotte Helgeland
Translated by: Zoë Chandler, Rebus Translations Avoin yhtiö

Stabenfeldt A/S, 2008
Fact checker: Charlotte Nagle, Horse Riding Instructor, BHS
Editor: Bobbie Chase
Printed in Italy

ISBN: 978-1-933343-87-7

Stabenfeldt, Inc.
457 North Main Street
Danbury, CT 06811
www.pony4kids.com

Available exclusively through PONY Book Club.

Contents

Introduction

Jumping is one of the world's most popular riding sports. What an amazing sight it is to watch a winning team of horse and rider clear fence after fence without a single mistake. A skillful rider and her agile mount moving as one. They soar with ease over even the trickiest fence.

It's taken both horse and rider a great deal of practice to get here. Luck can play a part in competitions – sometimes a horse will clip a pole, yet the pole won't fall out of the cups – but you won't jump a clear round on luck alone. Knowledge, skill and practice are the keys to jumping success. Although you won't become a good show jumper simply by reading books, you do need some book knowledge. Without it, you won't be able to put together safe training exercises, or jump safely either.

When I started riding, I never would have guessed that jumping would win my heart. At first, the horses were more important than anything else – just being around them and taking care of them. Jumping only began to interest me years later, when my first horse and I got to go to a camp led by a Show Jumping Champion from Finland, Kimmo Kinnunen. It was only then that I realized how important it is to have a basic understanding of a variety of jumping exercises. This fun and educational camp inspired me to learn show jumping theory – which has helped me ever since!

Nowadays, I compete in all the Olympic riding disciplines: dressage, show jumping and eventing. Training for and competing in jumping competitions takes up most of my time. The greatest thanks for this go to my gelding Gadfly, or Kalle as he's more affectionately known. Kalle loves jumping as much as I do, and has turned out to be even more talented than I expected. The sharp-eyed readers among you may spot Kalle in this book's illustrations. I'll give you a clue: Kalle is a rather large, copper chestnut – with a big white blaze!

I hope you spend many happy hours with this book, learning the theory behind jumping. If you enjoy reading it, you're already one step closer to achieving your goals!

1. Before you jump

At its best, show jumping is a fast and fabulous sport in which the course's different tasks test both horse and rider's skills and teamwork. Clearing a low fence isn't that difficult for either horse or rider. What makes it challenging is that you must keep your horse under control and on the aids at all times. And you have to be even more in control as the fences get higher. You must know exactly how to approach a fence. You must also control your horse's tempo – his speed – and move with the motion of the jump without disturbing him. And you have to keep all this in mind over the entire course.

When you're moving quickly, you don't have much time to think – your reactions must be instinctive. If your horse takes off for a jump from farther away than expected, you must immediately rise into a light seat, release the reins, and be prepared to go with the motion of a longer jump. Both horse and rider must learn many things before they can begin jumping. In the next chapter, we'll run through some of the most important ones.

This horse and rider team still have a lot to learn before they can begin jumping.

skills and exercises

The basic seat

Do you want to be a show jumper? Good! The first thing you have to learn is how to sit in a balanced, basic seat and be able to maintain it in all the gaits: walk, trot and canter. In the basic seat, your weight is evenly distributed in the saddle – you must sit evenly on both seat bones. Your legs rest relaxed against your horse's flanks. When the widest point of your foot – the ball – is in the stirrup, you'll find that your heel will lower itself almost automatically. Your hips face directly forward, but move with the horse's movements, both forward and backward. Your upper body is erect and also faces directly forward. Your posture is strong, yet relaxed. Viewed from the side, your shoulders, hips and heels form a straight vertical line. It's worth taking time to practice your seat, because your seat affects the use of all of your aids.

If a wizard were to make your horse disappear out from under you, you would land on your feet with your back straight and your knees flexed.

Forward driving aids

A horse is ridden forward, using your calves. When you want your horse to go forward, you squeeze gently with your calves. Your horse will react to the pressure. When your horse has responded to the aid, you can let your calves go back to resting lightly against his flanks. You should not maintain the calf squeeze for an extended period. If you do, your seat will no longer be relaxed and your horse will become numb to the aid.

You must also be able to ride in a basic seat with the shorter stirrups required for jumping.

Sounds easy, doesn't it? But horses are individuals and not all horses will react the same way to the aids you apply. A lively horse will start trotting when you merely think about squeezing your calves against his flanks. A more sedate horse may need several brisk squeezes and taps, or even a few clicks of the tongue, before he'll bother to take a single step. And the same horse may occasionally react differently to your aids. He might have his off days, just like you. Even though you usually enjoy riding, there may be some days when you're not exactly overjoyed at the prospect of going to the stables.

If your horse doesn't react to light pressure, give him a tap with your calves and click your tongue. If necessary, the calf aid can be reinforced by tapping your crop behind your calf. You should stop using the aid as soon as your horse reacts. Your seat must follow the motion.

Spurs may be used as an auxiliary aid, but only when you can keep your calf firmly in position. Spurs are not appropriate for beginners.

A lively horse will respond willingly to forward driving aids.

Holding aids

You hold a horse using the reins, your seat, or with voice aids like whoa or ho. Holding with the reins only involves the hands and forearms – the part of your arm above the elbow stays still. You move your fists back in a straight line toward your belly button and hips. You must stop holding your horse as soon as he reacts to the aid. Relax your arms and return to a normal light rein contact.

You can also reduce your horse's speed using your seat. First practice sitting to your horse's movements – let your hips move substantially in time to the rhythm of your horse's strides. When you want to hold your horse with your seat, reduce the movement of your hips and imagine that you are simply sitting still.

Use your imagination and a playground swing to improve your seat aid. When you want a swing to go higher, you push it with your hips. When you want to slow down, you simply sit still or put the brakes on by resisting the swing's motion with your hips.

A well-trained, obedient pony will obey his rider's commands without a fuss.

Turning aids

You turn a horse with both your reins and calves. Your seat aid – how your weight is distributed in the saddle – also plays a major role. A sensitive and well-trained horse will begin turning as soon as you direct your gaze and chest in the new direction. This is because your weight is shifting in the direction of the turn. The other turning aids are the inside rein and outside leg.

When you want to turn left, you should first look left. Next, pull carefully on the left-hand rein and shift your right calf forward, closer to the horse's ribs. Stop applying the aids as soon as your horse has responded to them.

Lateral aids

A leg yield is the term used for the motion in which a horse yields to your calves and steps sideways, crossing one leg over the other as it moves. During the leg yield, you can either keep your weight in the center of the saddle or shift it in the direction of the yield. Your other aids – the calf on the side of the leg yield and the reins – support the movement according to the kind of sidesteps you wish your horse to take. You can vary the angle of the leg yield, and there are many different types of leg yields that you can perform. Even though you won't do any leg yields when riding a course of jumps, practicing them can greatly benefit both you and your horse. You'll learn to control a combination of aids and get a better feel for your horse's movements and strides! When ridden correctly, leg yields will relax your horse and make his movements more fluid.

The angle of a leg yield shows how steeply you want your horse to step across his body.

Dressage for jumping

The ability to control your horse in both the indoor and outdoor arena is the foundation for all riding. That's why show jumpers must also be diligent when it comes to practicing their dressage skills. Dressage for jumping combines dressage exercises with poles, single bars, or small fences. Dressage for jumping allows you to practice the techniques, seats and aids required for jumping. Both horse and rider are then better able to concentrate on the technical side of jumping and can "dry run" the skills required for jumping a course.

The long release

When jumping, it's important to know how to move with the motion of the jump. Yes, there are a couple of things you'll have to practice before going over your first fence – like the long release and light seat. By releasing the reins, you'll make sure that you don't jerk your horse's mouth as he jumps. There are three releases that you can use when jumping: the **long release, short release**, and **automatic release.**

In the long release, you hold the reins in the usual way with fists softly closed. To begin the long release, slide both hands along your horse's mane toward his ears. When you reach the halfway point, press your fists lightly against your horse's neck. You can also catch a lock of mane under each thumb. The reins will now remain loose between your hands and the bit, allowing your horse plenty of room to move his head with the jump. When your hands are "anchored" to the mane, they're also more likely to remain in the correct position, which in turn will keep you from tugging on the reins. To end the long release, slide your hands back evenly and resume normal rein contact.

The long release can be learned right from your very first lead rein lessons, by riding over poles, for example. It's also a vital skill for experienced riders who are training young horses to jump. An inexperienced horse may make enormous leaps over his first fences – so it's a good idea (even for experienced hands) to take a little extra support from the mane.

The short release

As its name suggests, the short release is shorter than the long release, but is in principle the same. You'll also need the short release for exercises involving low fences, single bars, and poles.

The automatic release

This is a tough one even for really experienced riders! In the automatic release, you maintain a light rein contact throughout the jump. Your hands slide "automatically" toward the horse's mouth – you only give your horse exactly the amount of rein he needs for the jump. You need to use a really gentle touch, paying very close attention to your horse's movements.

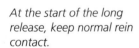

At the start of the long release, keep normal rein contact.

During the long release, slide your fists along the mane.

You can also grab a lock of mane during the release. This will help keep your hands in the correct position.

Even inexperienced riders can practice the long release.

The light, or two-point, seat

There are two types of "light" seat: the actual light, or two-point, seat and the full, or three-point, seat. To rise into the light seat, you first move your bottom slightly backwards in the saddle and put more weight into the stirrups. You then raise your bottom completely out of the saddle and shift your weight entirely into the stirrups – onto two points. It's important to keep your calves firmly in position and

Really experienced riders are able to maintain light rein contact throughout the automatic release.

ensure that your upper body leans only very slightly forward. You must remain balanced in the stirrups. You may turn your toes slightly upwards, so that your knee and thigh are not pressed against the saddle. Remember that wizard we imagined during the basic seat? If your horse were to suddenly disappear from under you, you would remain stable and land on your feet with your knees flexed.

You must always maintain your balance in relation to the ground – your horse just happens to be between your legs at the moment.

In the light seat, your bottom is out of the saddle.

Problems with the light seat

The rider's calf is too far back. Her upper body then leans too far forward, and both her knee and thigh are pressed against the saddle.

The rider's leg is thrust forward. She is no longer balanced in the stirrups and her bottom will fall back into the saddle.

The rider's toes are turned inward. This shifts her weight from the stirrups onto her knee and thigh, and her calf will no longer remain in the correct position. Her feet may come entirely out of the stirrups when jumping.

The full, or three-point, seat

In the full seat, your weight is distributed over three points: both stirrups and your bottom. However, you don't press your bottom deep into the saddle as you would for a basic dressage seat. Instead, you lightly hold it just above the saddle with at least half of your weight in the stirrups. The full seat is used between fences and when riding over poles.

Skillful riders can maintain their balance in the basic, full and light seats as well as in all conceivable forms in between! When jumping a course, you have to be able to use and change between these seats as the situation demands.

In the full seat, your bottom will only lightly touch the saddle.

21

The leading rein

Before jumping, it's also worth practicing how to use the leading rein. Even if you know how to turn your horse in the standard manner – by pulling the rein slightly backwards – you won't be able to do that in mid-jump. Remember: you have to release the reins while going over a fence. Therefore, in addition to your leg and seat aids, you'll have to use the leading rein. Move your hand out to the side in the direction you wish the horse to turn. When turning left, the left hand – slightly led by its pinky finger edge – moves straight out to the left-hand side. The leading rein can also be used when turning into a fence, but it is most helpful in mid-jump. You won't need this technique during your very first jumping lessons, but it will be necessary when you start jumping courses. If you need to change direction over a fence, you must let your horse know where to go next while he's still in the air.

You use a leading rein for turning on a show jumping course.

When jumping against the clock, the winners are often those riders who know how to turn their horse into the next fence while still going over the previous one. This is when you need the leading rein!

Train your eyes

Focusing on where you're headed next plays a major role in jumping. If you don't look at a fence, you won't be able to make a precise approach or judge the correct take-off distance.

Train your eyes whenever you ride. When riding over poles, look at the pole you're approaching. When in the arena, always turn your gaze to the next side while you're still halfway down the previous one. If you're riding dressage figures, look at the letter you're heading for. When out on a trail ride, always look at the next tree stump, the next branch in the path, the next shadow on the ground, etc. And it's vital to really look, not just glance, at them.

Think about hitting a baseball with a bat. You follow the ball as it's pitched so that you can hit it with your bat. If you glance at your watch, you probably won't hit the ball – unless you're really, really lucky!

Double posting

Double posting is a fun but challenging exercise to help you improve both your light seat and your balance. You'll also enhance your sense of rhythm and increase your muscular strength. You usually post to the trot on every second stride. When double posting, you rise for two strides in a row before sitting down. The rhythm of a normal posting trot is up-down-up-down. The rhythm for double posting is up-up-down-up-up-down. You can't maintain a light seat for two strides in a row unless your calves and upper body are in the correct position. This is a great way to check your balance!

With practice, you can manage a variety of different posting trot sequences. Vary the number of strides you take in a light seat and the number you take sitting in the saddle.

During double posting, you maintain a light seat for two strides in a row.

Transitions and changes of tempo

You can use transitions to help your mount listen to and obey you better. You'll also learn to adapt the strength and application of your aids to both the situation and your horse. Make transitions between the gaits. Although transitions are usually practiced in a basic seat, you can also make them harder by trying them in a light seat. This challenging exercise can help you maintain a solid seat even during tempo changes.

Tempo means speed – how many feet a horse covers in a certain time. Transitions within a gait are called changes of tempo. Start with a standard walk in the basic seat. Shorten your horse's walking stride as much as you can without causing him to halt. Once you've gotten the hang of shortening your horse's stride, try lengthening it as much as possible without your horse breaking into a trot. End the exercise by returning to a normal walk. You can practice these transitions in all gaits. Why not try them in a light seat, too?

Tempo = speed
(horse feet/minute)

You have to keep smiling, even when traveling at high speed.

skills and exercises

What does your horse need to know before you can jump him? You can't just lasso a mustang in the prairie and enter him in the next show jumping competition. You begin a foal's training by getting him used to being handled and cared for – standing while haltered, brushing, leading, shoeing, traveling and tacking up, etc. These basics are the same for all young horses no matter what their future careers will be.

Yet your horse still has a long way to go before he becomes a show jumper. He must learn a ton of new things before he can jump his first fence with you on his back. You can only begin riding a horse when he is about three years old. But before this, it's a good idea to get a future show jumper acquainted with loose jumping, ground-driving and longe-reining. All of these will benefit your horse's basic training later on.

Training a foal is always a job for an experienced horsewoman. But you'll learn a lot by following the process.

Will I be a show jumper when I grow up?

Loose jumping

For loose jumping, you'll need either an indoor arena or an outdoor arena with a wall high enough to prevent the loose horse from escaping. An indoor arena often makes for a better and more tranquil setting. Your horse will not be able to see other horses through the walls and will concentrate better on the task at hand. Outside, he may be able to see over the fence and become distracted by other horses in their stalls or in the stable yard. A really talented horse may even view the arena's perimeter fence as a jump and soar easily over even a high railing.

Set up your fences in a lane along the long side so that they can be jumped on the left rein. The lane can be constructed using standards and poles, or by fixing easily detachable tape or rope between the standards. In some arenas, a ready-built lane can be lowered into place from a storage space in the ceiling. The lane can go around the whole arena, or simply guide your horse down the long side to the fences. The fences are placed along the lane so that your horse cannot get past them on either side.

Loose jumping in an indoor arena.

If there are mirrors in the arena, they should be covered with, for example, blankets. A loose jumping horse can accidentally run into a mirror in which it sees movement.

When loose jumping, you must always be aware of your horses' ability and match the fences to his training level and **jumping capacity** – his skill level. In addition to the lane and fences, you'll need trained and appropriately dressed assistants, longe whips, and a pail of oats. Some trainers loose jump mares and their unweaned foals together over small fences. Young horses, two- or three-year-olds in particular, will loose jump in a variety of shows and training events. Figure 1 shows an example of a loose jumping lane.

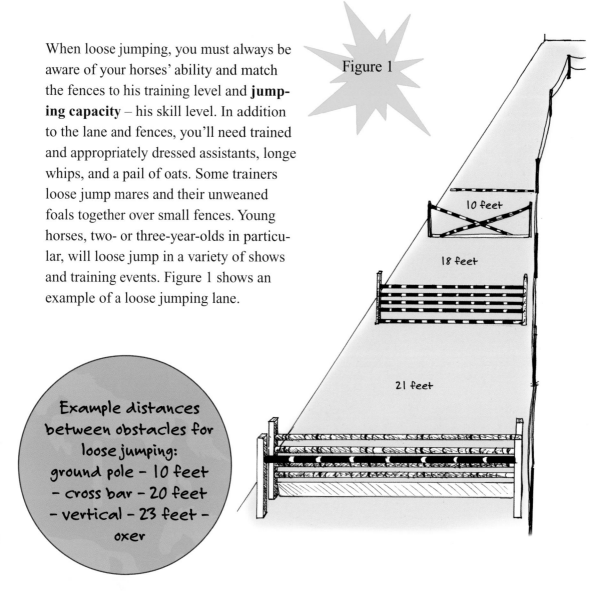

Figure 1

10 feet

18 feet

21 feet

Example distances between obstacles for loose jumping: ground pole – 10 feet – cross bar – 20 feet – vertical – 23 feet – oxer

An inexperienced horse must be introduced to loose jumping gradually. At first, simply leading your horse along the lane can be enough. You can then teach him to run through the lane by letting him free just before the long side and stopping him with a tempting pail of oats at the end. This trick works on many horses. Even a sedate horse can get enthusiastic about jumping when he knows he'll be getting

some oats at the end. And an enthusiastic jumper can be difficult to stop without giving him a good reason. You must be able to stop your horse when required at the end of the lane. During the break, you can rearrange the obstacles in the lane.

When your horse has become accustomed to the lane itself, you can place poles in the position for the upcoming jumps. Add poles one at a time. Only proceed with the next phase when your horse has gotten the hang of the previous one. Check that the distances are suitable for your horse. There should be one canter stride between poles. Fences should also be built one by one: after the ground pole comes a cross bar, after the cross bar a vertical, and then finally after the vertical comes an oxer. Your horse must be able to clear each fence without fault before moving onto the next one!

A horse in basic condition can only be loose jumped down a lane about ten times in one session. Before this, you must warm him up with walking and trotting exercises, either on the longe or loose in the arena. And don't forget the walking and cool down at the end! During your first session, you probably won't have

time for even one fence. Later, once your horse is more experienced, you can begin with a small fence and move on to larger ones. But it's still a good idea to finish with an easy fence. If the final oxer in the lane has been set high, it's worth lowering it for the final round. This way, your horse doesn't get the idea that each new round always requires greater effort.

Ground-driving

When training a harness horse, ground-driving is absolutely necessary, and it doesn't hurt to include it in the training of a future saddle horse, too. When ground-driving, you don't sit in a carriage, but instead, simply walk behind the horse. You can begin ground-driving as soon as your horse is accustomed to being led in a bridle. You'll need two people at first: a driver, plus someone to lead the horse

when necessary. The driver holds long driving reins. These reins are threaded through handholds on a belt that the horse wears on its back. The driver and leader guide the horse forward by clicking their tongues. They reduce his speed using voice aids and gentle pulling on the reins, and also teach him to turn in the direction of the rein being pulled by the driver. Once the horse understands the meaning of these aids, the leader is no longer required. The horse learns the rein and voice aids, and also to move forward on his own.

Ground-driving can make a nice change even for a saddle horse with more training under his belt. Skillful trainers use it to teach their horses some really challenging moves. You may have seen pictures of riders at the Spanish Riding School in Vienna ground-driving their superb white Lipizzaners and getting them to perform some truly top-notch moves. We'll be happy with a lot less from our young horse, but it's worth considering whether a competent harness trainer could also school your future mount as a harness horse. A horse can pull a light carriage even before he's able to work with a saddle.

Longe-reining

Longe-reining teaches a young horse to travel in a circle and obey voice aids. The longeur (person who is longing, or lunging, the horse) stands in the middle of the circle holding the longe rein. The other end of the longe rein is attached to the horse's bit or longe cavesson – a bridle without a bit. In the longeur's other hand is the longe whip. Seen from above, the longeur stands at the point of an isoceles triangle. The triangle's long sides are made up by the longe rein and the whip. The horse forms the short side. The longeur may need someone to help lead the horse during its first longe-reining sessions. Once the horse has learned to listen to the longeur and stay in a balanced circle, the helper is no longer necessary.

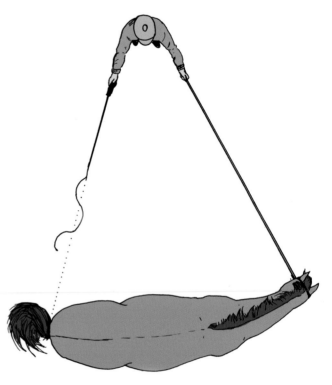

Your horse will learn the voice aids during longe-reining: clicking the tongue drives your horse forward while a calm "whoa" or "ho" slows him down. Gait transitions can be taught with the commands walk, trot and canter. When moving up to a faster pace, the command is given sharply and you help your horse understand by clicking your tongue. The command should be uttered more calmly when moving down to a slower pace. Teaching your horse voice commands will be of benefit later when breaking him in. When your novice mount is accustomed to having a saddle on his back – both when stationary and being led – it's a good idea to longe-rein him with the saddle on. Your horse will then get used to carrying the saddle while he's moving. You should, however, remove the stirrups during the early stages of his training, otherwise their swinging might spook him.

Breaking in

Through loose jumping, ground-driving and longe-reining, your future mount will have learned a whole range of the skills required for him to be ridden. When a horse trusts his trainer, getting into the saddle for the first time doesn't generally pose problems. But don't just leap carelessly into the saddle without warning, or you may spook the horse. You'll also need an experienced assistant to hold your horse the first time you mount. Practice mounting your horse by gradually placing weight onto his back. Many young horses take their first steps with their trainer lying sideways across their backs on her belly. You have to read your horse's reactions so that you know when it's the right time to move on to the next phase. Once your horse is confident about having weight on his back, you can sit up in the saddle. At first, you should steer your horse using just voice and rein aids – calf aids will be taught later.

A young horse starting out with his training is called a rookie.

Basic schooling

Basic schooling can begin once a trainer is able to safely control her rookie without the need for an assistant. Your horse will be at least three years old by this time. Your rookie will now learn the aids used by a rider. In principle, your horse can be taught to respond to any aids whatsoever. The ones usually used are detailed in the section The Rider: skills and exercises. Teaching your horse these aids will enable him to be ridden by other people too, and not just his trainer. Your horse can be considered to have completed his basic schooling once he accepts rein contact in all the gaits and responds to the forward driving, holding, turning and lateral aids.

Poles and fences

During basic schooling, you can start to familiarize your horse with poles, single bars and fences – even with a rider in the saddle. It's best if your horse has first been loose jumped. You shouldn't introduce too many new things at once when training a horse. So set up your horse's first ground poles in a place where he can move in a relaxed, straight line without difficulty. The familiar long side next to the wall or railing is an ideal place. Some trainers use

A horse that has completed his basic schooling will accept rein contact and make the movements asked of him, but not necessarily submissively.

the same place where the horse was previously loose jumped. When your horse is clearing poles successfully, you can begin replacing the poles with fences. Set up fences one at a time, just as you did during loose jumping. Once your horse has found his balance in this exercise, it's time to move on to fences in other locations.

Distances between ground poles:

– trot poles about 4 ½ feet apart
– canter poles about 10-12 feet apart

Start with just a single pole. Always use three or more poles for a sequence – if there are only two, your horse may try to jump them both at once.

Clearing the trotting poles with ease.

Oops! What happened here? The horse was supposed to trot over the single bars - not jump!

This looks great: this is how you should ride over the trotting poles.

Your horse's first fences should not be too high. They should be sufficiently wide and equipped with good wings to steer your young horse clearly into the jump. A good practical tip is to place a ground pole about 4 inches in front of a fence. It will help your horse judge the height and placement of the fence.

Begin with a straight approach to fences. Trot or canter your horse on a straight line both before and after the fence. Only later should you practice a curved approach. A "draft horse" can be used to draw a timid young horse over jumps. If an older and more experienced horse leads, a young rookie will normally follow willingly. Following the herd! That's the way it is with horses and other animals with a strong herd instinct.

Your horse's first fences should be wide, low and equipped with wings. More demanding fences should only be jumped by horses with more advanced training.

An inexperienced jumper may make an over-long jump arc.

When training your horse to jump, it's vital that he remains confident in his abilities. So with an inexperienced horse, it's a good idea to stick to exercises that are both easy and fun for him. Just one failure could severely set back your horse's training. This is a danger with timid and sensitive horses in particular.

2. Jumping equipment

Standard riding gear is sufficient for jumping. That means you'll need a riding helmet and, preferably, riding pants, gloves and boots. Your horse will need a saddle and bridle, plus the required protective gear. It's also a good idea to invest in some safety gear, such as a safety vest and safety stirrups.

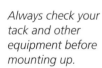

Always check your tack and other equipment before mounting up.

Equipment for the rider

You should use an ASTM/SEI approved riding helmet for jumping. When buying your helmet, be sure to check that it meets the required standards. You'll usually find the marking inside the helmet. A safety helmet must fit snugly and be undamaged. Your helmet could fall down over your eyes during a jump if it's too large or the wrong shape. Your helmet shouldn't be uncomfortably tight, but it shouldn't wobble around when you move your head either.

A pair of grippy **riding gloves** ensures a firm but gentle grip on the reins. Bare hands can easily get blisters from the reins – another good reason to wear gloves. And they'll also keep your hands warm in cold weather.

Riding pants are close-fitting and stretchy. They don't have any thick internal seams. The patches cover either the inner knee area alone, or both the inner knee area and the bottom and thighs. Many people prefer full seat riding pants, because they offer more support and stability in the saddle. Others prefer riding pants equipped only with knee patches – for show jumping in particular. When rising into a light seat, these pants allow you to slide your bottom backwards in the saddle a lot easier than full seat ones will.

Jodhpurs are riding pants that are intended for use with short jodhpur boots. Think carefully before you start using jodhpurs,

as these cannot be worn with long riding boots.

Your ankles come under a lot of strain in the light seat, so good footwear is essential. A pair of correctly fitted **long riding boots** will provide the best support for your ankles. A jumping boot may have a slightly shorter and softer leg than a dres-

sage boot. You ride with shorter stirrups when jumping, so a boot that's too long could dig into the back of your knee.

Not everyone enjoys riding in long boots. Some people prefer to ride in **short jodhpur boots.** When using short boots, it's a good idea to wear **gaiters** or **minichaps** – they'll provide extra support for you and protection for your horse's hair. If your woolen socks or leggings chafe against your horse's flank, his hairs may get stuck between the stitches and pulled out.

~~~~~~~~~~

A good riding jacket and shirt are always stretchy, close-fitting and suitable for the weather conditions you'll be riding in. Billowing hems and flapping hoods will get in the way when you're riding. They can also be dangerous, as they can get caught on something or spook your horse. When approaching a fence, you have to rise into a light seat and release the reins. Your clothing must really stretch well to enable you to slide your hands far enough forward. Riding jackets usually have exceptionally long sleeves and are cut to allow as much movement as possible around the back and shoulders. A long-sleeved top is better than a sleeveless one even in warm weather. The sleeves will protect your arms from being scratched by branches when you're out on the trail. And if you do fall, you'll minimize your risk of getting skinned. Long sleeves will also protect you from sunburn and horse-fly bites.

A variety of boots with grooved soles have been designed for show jumping! You use them with rubber stirrup boots that have a matching tread. The rubber boots slot into the grooves and help your feet to remain solidly in the stirrups.

Your jacket should be close-fitting and stretchy, so it doesn't prevent you from moving with the motion of your horse's jump.

The show jumper's **crop** is shorter than those used in dressage. An overly long crop may accidentally flick the horse when you release the reins. Show jumping competition rules also define a maximum length for crops. When choosing a crop, make sure you can get a firm grip on the handle. Although using the wrist strap will ensure your crop doesn't fall to the ground, it makes quick changes of hand tricky.

Practice using your crop so that, when necessary, you can also tap it behind your calf when jumping a fence.

Going riding. Which of these riders is most suitably dressed for jumping?

Think very carefully before using **spurs**. You may accidentally jab your horse's flank if your calves don't remain in exactly the right position during a jump. Spurs are an aid for experienced riders only.

Although **safety vests**, also known as **body protectors**, have been designed for use in show jumping and cross-country in particular, you can wear them whenever you're around horses. You can't be sure that you'll stay in the saddle and you never know when you could be kicked or knocked down. A safety vest will protect your upper body if you fall. It covers areas containing vital organs. Although a safety vest is no guarantee you won't get hurt, it reduces the risk of serious injury if you happen to fall. There are different kinds of safety vests available and a variety of safety ratings. Ask for help in trying on and choosing your safety vest. Your vest should feel comfortable and fit properly, otherwise it will probably sit in the closet gathering dust.

Tack

Have you ever wondered why horses need tack? The answer is simple: to help riders use their aids and to improve their balance when mounted. Tack also protects your horse from bruises. A **saddle** and **bridle** are the minimum tack required for jumping. Without these, you won't be allowed to compete. **Protective boots** are not compulsory, but are worth using if your horse brushes or steps on his heels. In addition to the basic tack, some specialized equipment has also been designed for jumping.

The **jump saddle** has been specially designed for jumping. It has a long, shallow seat. Its saddle flaps are short and the knee rolls are placed in an extreme forward position. This type of saddle provides the best support for the light seat. It's difficult to ride with short stirrups in a **dressage saddle,** which has a deeper seat and longer saddle flaps. But a jump saddle makes it difficult to sit well in a basic seat. Good saddles are always quite expensive. If you do both dressage and jumping but don't have the means to buy specialized saddles for both, it's worth choosing an **all-purpose saddle**. Its seat and saddle flaps inhabit the middle ground between the dressage and jump saddles, making it a suitable substitute for both.

An all-purpose saddle can be used for both jumping and dressage.

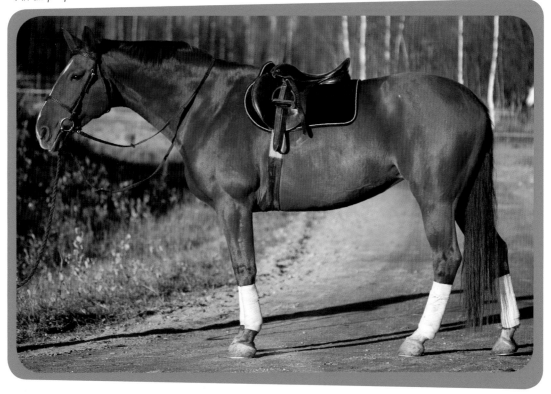

It's difficult to ride in a light seat when using a dressage saddle.

The jump saddle has a shallow seat. This one has a belly guard girth.

Always ask an experienced horseperson for help when fitting a saddle. You should also take your saddle to a saddler for regular maintenance. A badly fitting saddle, or one with worn flocking, can cause your horse painful knocks and even muscle trouble.

You'll also need some additional saddle accessories: a **girth**, a **saddle blanket**, and **safety stirrup irons** and **leathers**. There are a variety of different safety stirrups available. All are designed to ensure that your foot does not get stuck in the iron if you happen to fall. Remember to check the stitching on your stirrup leathers regularly, as a leather that breaks over a fence means trouble!

The outer edges of these stirrup irons are equipped with rubber bands. If your foot is stuck in the stirrup, this rubber band will stretch or break.

Many show jumpers need a **belly guard** attached to their girth. When jumping, some horses bring the soles of their front hooves very close to their bellies. The belly guard will protect your horse's belly from hoof strikes. Its use is also recommended if your horse has studded shoes. When the belly guard is integrated into the girth, it is called a **belly guard girth.**

Horses used for show jumping and eventing often wear a **grackle**, also known as a figure-eight noseband. This model allows plenty of room between the noseband and the corners of your horse's mouth, so they don't get pinched between the bit and the noseband. A grackle won't slide down over your horse's nostrils either.

There are many kinds of **bits**. The most commonly used is the **snaffle**. A snaffle's mouthpiece is made from two or more parts connected by joints. A bit should be undamaged, the correct size for your horse, and suitable for the type of riding you'll be doing. Different bits will have a different effect on your horse. For your own safety, a lively horse may require a stronger bit over a more sedate and obedient one. Horses with sensitive mouths will work best with a **rubber straight bar bit** or a **rounded three-piece snaffle.** For hot-blooded horses, you may decide to choose a **pessoa bit** with a cheekpiece. You'll also find bridles without bits – the **hackamore** is the one most often used for jumping.

A grackle noseband with a snaffle bit.

Always check competition rules in advance to determine which bits are allowed.

Snaffle bits may have cheekpieces that will enhance the effect of the leading rein.

You can also use **auxiliary reins** when show jumping. They should, however, be of a type that doesn't restrict your horse's head in any way while it's jumping. You can therefore completely forget both the **side reins** used in longe-reining and the **standing martingale,** which prevents a horse from tossing its head in the air. The **running martingale**, on the other hand, is a familiar sight on jumpers. Although it won't prevent your horse from lifting or lowering its head, it will enhance rein contact through diagonal pressure if your horse throws its muzzle skyward. Eventers in particular use a **breast collar,** which prevents the saddle from sliding backwards during a jump. When the breast collar and martingale are combined as one piece of tack, you get a **breast collar-martingale**.

A breast collar-martingale. See page 42 for correct alignment.

Ask your instructor for advice when using auxiliary reins, and always remember to check competition rules in advance to make sure they're permitted.

If your horse brushes – catches the inside of his leg with the opposite leg – he will need **brushing boots. Tendon boots** are worn on the forelegs when jumping. As your horse's forelegs hit the ground when he lands from a jump, his flexor tendons are in danger of being knocked by his rear hooves. That's why tendon boots have a reinforced panel running down the back. They also provide protection against brushing.

You should use **bell boots** if your horse overreaches so that his rear hooves step lightly on his front heels. Bell boots cover the hoof and are made from either rubber or neoprene. Rubber bell boots that can be pulled over the hooves tend to stay on better. If riding in an indoor or outdoor arena, you can also choose bell boots that fasten with velcro. This means you don't have to lift the hoof to put on the boots. Getting pullover bell boots onto your horse can be a sweaty job, and you're in danger of catching your fingertips between the boot and the hoof.

Neoprene boots have been developed especially for eventing. They cover your horse's whole cannon bone right down to the hollow of the heel, providing support for both pastern and tendons. If going over cross-country fences, it's a good idea to reinforce velcro boot fastenings with duct tape. Velcro is more likely to come undone accidentally if it gets wet during a water jump. If you can't get hold of suitable protection, you can use leg wraps or pads until you do. Proper protectors will, however, offer better protection than leg wraps – and will definitely be easier to put on and take off.

Tendon boots protect your horse when he's jumping.

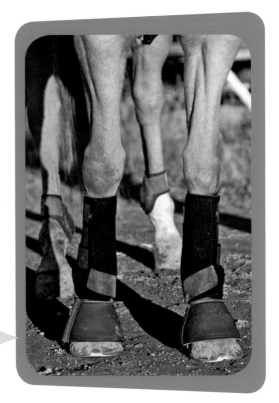

On the forelegs: neoprene boots and bell boots. On the hind legs: short brushing boots.

47

3. Show jumping

When show jumping, horse and rider work as a team. Their task is to clear the obstacles on the course as quickly and with as few mistakes as possible. Penalty points, called faults, are given for knocking down fences. Faults are also given for refusals – stopping before a fence – or for running out of either side of an obstacle. Show jumping demands a lot of skill from the rider, and a show jumping mount must be obedient and agile.

The outward appearance of obstacles may vary greatly and they may include some of the elements seen in eventing. However, unlike event fences, the top part of a show jumping fence is always dislodgeable. Particularly bright fences or a challenging combination can pose difficulties for an inexperienced horse-and-rider team. It's not simply a question of who can jump the highest fence. Clearing a single fence cleanly is not enough – you have to be able to cope with a number of fences in a row.

Types of show jumping obstacles

Obstacles can be placed into categories based on their appearance. The two main

Fences in a sand arena.

categories are: **verticals** and **spreads**. Fences can also be set up to form **combinations** and **related lines**. There will be one or two canter strides between the fences in a combination. A related line will have at least three canter strides between fences. A **special obstacle** may be distinctly narrower than any other fence on the course, or an exceptional color. What would you think – not to mention what would your horse think – of a wall that was painted to look like a dragon? The special obstacle category may also include familiar elements from eventing. Once you can recognize the different types of fences and know the theory behind clearing them, you can start jumping them in practice, too.

Verticals

Verticals are built from two standards with either poles, planks or a gate between them. You can also place fillers under them, such as water trays, brush boxes or hay bales. Choose the cups you attach to the standards according to the dislodgeable element: curved cups suit poles while straight cups are used with gates. A wall is another typical type of vertical. Instead of the usual pole, its dislodgeable element usually consists of light blocks.

Approach a vertical in a normal, rhythmical canter. Keep your eyes trained on the center of the uppermost pole. You will

A wall is a typical type of vertical.

then be able to judge the correct take-off distance. The take-off point should be at a distance in front of the fence that is equal to the fence's height. In theory, jumping verticals is easy, because your horse doesn't need to jump very far. Of course, a horse can never simply jump upwards – its jump will always take it forward, too. If your horse approaches a fence in a canter that is too long and low, it's likely that he'll take off from too far away, causing a flat jump arc. A canter that is too short will result in your horse taking off too close to the fence and he won't necessarily have time to reach the apex of his jump before the highest point of the fence. Both an overly short or overly long take-off to a vertical will almost certainly lead to tumbling poles. Verticals can therefore be quite challenging to jump. You must be in control of your horse and keep him in a short but impulsive canter. Verticals primarily require precision.

Did we forget cross bars? Of course not! Cross bars make for excellent practice fences. They guide horse and rider into jumping a fence at its center. You won't see cross bars at major show jumping competitions because competition rules require a standard at both ends of every pole. Some minor competitions may run a cross bars class for beginners. But imagine what it would be like to approach a 4-foot high cross bar!

A cross bar guides horse and rider to jump the fence at its center.

Spreads

A **spread** with two elements is called an oxer. You will need four standards to build one. Set up the lower vertical element first. Add a second pair of standards immediately behind the first element. You'll need to attach **safety cups** to one of the poles. Safety cups will release and drop the pole straight down if your horse's hooves knock it from above. Safety cups are used for the rear element of a spread. If your horse doesn't jump far enough, or his rear legs hit the pole from above, the cup will release and drop the pole directly downward. Check that the pole on the rearmost element – the back rail – is not lower than the front one.

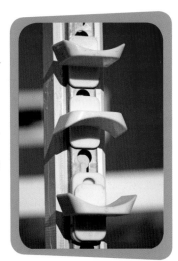

The top cup is suitable for poles, the center one for planks and gates, and the bottom one is a safety cup.

A parallel oxer's back rail is set at the same height as its front rail. The back rail of an ascending oxer is about 4 inches higher than its front rail.

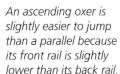

An ascending oxer is slightly easier to jump than a parallel because its front rail is slightly lower than its back rail.

A **triple bar** has three elements and requires six standards. Seen from the side, the fence looks long and gradually increases in height like a staircase. The front rail is lowest, the middle rail slightly higher, and the back rail the highest.

Your horse will need to take off close to a triple bar. A very long take-off will require your horse to really stretch into the jump if he's to get his hind legs cleanly over it. When approaching a triple bar, focus on the top pole of the foremost element and estimate the required take-off distance. Imagine that the triple bar is a vertical of the same height as its front rail, but approach it with a slightly more vigorous canter. Jumping a triple bar requires courage, strength and foresight from both horse and rider.

> **How are show jumps measured?**
> **Height:** measure from the ground to the upper edge of the dislodgeable element.
> **Width:** the width of the dislodgeable element = the length of the pole.
> **Spread:** from the front edge of the front rail to the back edge of the back rail.

Clearing a triple bar requires a lengthy jump.

Combinations

Combinations comprise two or three fences. The first element in a double is referred to as A and the second as B. A triple has the elements A, B and C. Although there is more than one fence, it's worth thinking of a combination as a single obstacle. The fences in a combination are usually either verticals or oxers. There are normally one or two canter strides between fences. Fences without canter strides in between are called **bounce combinations** and are classed as special obstacles in show jumping.

At a show jumping competition, if your horse refuses elements B or C in a combination, you have to jump the entire combination again. Although a combination is composed of multiple elements, the rules consider it a single obstacle.

Doubles may already appear in easy show jumping classes. Triples are usually only found at more demanding levels. Combinations are challenging because a bad approach to element A will most likely affect how you take elements B and C. If your horse goes into element A with a long take-off, you'll easily find yourself too close to element B. A short take-off point to the first fence can lead to an angular jump, and your horse may not be able to lengthen his stride to correctly cover the distance to the next fence. A straight approach is also important. A diagonal line over element A will almost always send you rapidly past, instead of over, element B.

The distance between fences in a combination plays a major role in how easy they are to clear. The box below shows the basic distances to keep in mind when building practice combinations.

Distances between fences in a combination (for horse):

one canter stride combinations (vertical-vertical)
fence height 2 feet – distance between fences 20 feet
fence height 2 ½ feet – distance between fences 20 ½ feet
fence height 3 feet – distance between fences 21 feet
Take 4 inches off above distances for larger ponies, and 8 inches off for smaller ponies/horses.

two canter stride combinations (vertical-oxer)
fence height 2 feet – distance between fences 32 feet
fence height 2 ¾ feet – distance between fences 32 ½ feet
fence height 3 ¼ feet – distance between fences 33 feet
Take 4 inches off above distances for larger ponies/horses, and 8 inches off for smaller ponies.

Related lines

There will be at least three canter strides between the fences in a related line. The fences are, however, so close together that they cannot be ridden as single fences – you must start thinking about your approach to the second fence while you're clearing the first one. Related lines are usually divisible by the length of a horse's stride – 12 feet. Even if you aren't very interested in math, you're going to need it for jumping.

Distances between fences in a related line:
48 feet = 3 canter strides
60 feet = 4 canter strides
72 feet = 5 canter strides.

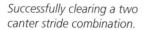

Successfully clearing a two canter stride combination.

54

You might be wondering how 48 feet can possibly equal three canter strides. When you divide 48 feet by the length of one canter stride – 12 feet – you get 4! You're quite correct of course, but in practice you have to take into account the distance your horse covers while landing from one fence and taking off for the next. That's why we've added an "extra" 12 feet.

If your horse's canter stride is usually a lot longer or shorter than 12 feet, you should make precise plans on how you'll ride over related lines. Ponies will easily take six canter strides over 72 feet. If you ride a long-striding horse over the same distance, you should try to shorten its canter stride so that it doesn't try to take off after only four strides.

Special obstacles

What is a special obstacle? No one can give you a perfect answer to that question. If you only jump standard pole fences in your home arena, your horse could consider a bright red wall to be a very special obstacle indeed. At jumping competitions, a special obstacle is classed as one that differs substantially from the other obstacles on the course. Let's go through a few of the fences we haven't mentioned yet. We'll call these our special obstacles.

A **wave plank** is a plank that's used as a dislodgeable element in a show jump. It's special because, as its name suggests, it's shaped to look like a wave. If the crest of the wave is at the center, you don't want to jump it there. The lowest point of the wave is the best place to jump. Be precise when aiming for the bottom of the wave, otherwise your horse may accidentally run out of the jump.

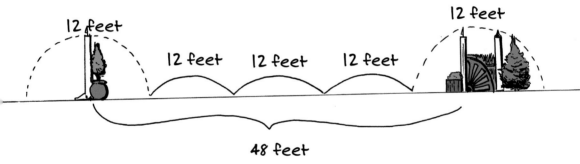

A blue tarp acts as a "water tray" underneath this wave plank fence.

You must approach a **narrow fence** with care. Shorten your horse's canter so that he is completely under your control. Keep your horse's barrel straight and approach the jump with your undivided attention.

An **airy fence** may only have one pole. Without a ground line, it's more difficult for your horse to estimate the height of the jump and judge the correct take-off point. Approach the fence very precisely

This narrow fence is quite airy.

and make sure that your horse gets a clear look at it while he's still a good distance away. He'll then realize it's a fence and won't just canter straight through the pole. Judging the correct take-off distance for this type of fence requires a lot of skill.

Brightly colored fences may scare you more than they do your horse, as you see colors in a different way. Remember to practice jumping fences of many different colors. You can make a standard vertical more exotic by draping a colorful old blanket across it.

Show jumping courses may also contain **familiar elements from eventing**, such as the **water tray**. You can get your horse accustomed to water trays by practicing with a folded tarp. First place it under the fence in a tight roll. Once your horse is used to this, gradually widen the tarp. Your horse will soon be jumping the tarp without a care – even when you've poured a tubful of water onto it!

Over the fences

The previous section contained some advice on how to jump different types of fences. Now let's think about what you can do as a rider to ensure that your horse makes as clean and as balanced a jump as possible.

In theory, your role is straightforward: you have to set up the situation for a successful jump without disturbing your horse. Putting this into practice is, however, another thing entirely. Start by learning to feel your horse's movements and reactions as if they were part of your own body. Your horse must obey your aids immediately. Also practice judging distances. If you canter toward a fence at a certain tempo, will you take off at the correct distance? Should you shorten the canter if your current take-off point appears to be too close to the fence? And can you ride forward if your last canter stride looks to be falling short of the fence? Luckily your horse can also judge his take-off point. When you ride skillfully and carefully, you'll assist him greatly in this challenging task.

Lines

Let's start by establishing the lines to be ridden over the fences. Yes, it all starts with such an elementary topic! If a fence is only 10 feet wide, you can't afford to steer your horse in any old direction. A straight approach toward the center of a fence is called a **straight line**.

A straight line is just like the straight line you'd draw on paper with a ruler. Straight lines in the arena are usually located along the long sides. They're good places to put, for example, combinations or related distances. Sounds easy, doesn't it? If your horse moves in a very straight line and remains under your control, riding a straight line is fairly simple. But things

Both horse and rider look directly forward when taking a straight line.

start to get complicated if you have a very lively horse. During a long straight, your horse can get excited and become hard to handle. Don't underestimate fences on a straight line – remember to ride every stride with care.

A straight line may lead you **diagonally** over a fence. Yes, you did read that correctly! Make sure that your horse's neck and barrel are straight. The fence will be at a 45-degree angle to you as you clear it. Practice diagonal approaches too, but only once you've gotten the hang of a standard approach on all lines. When you've mastered this technique, you'll be able to win jump-offs with amazing times.

An exercise for riding a straight line

Place one ground pole on the inside of the track at the mid-point of the long side. Approach it on both reins and in all gaits. Make sure to always ride a straight line to the poles. Your horse's neck and barrel should also remain straight at all times. Horses often try to drift onto the track. Keep your horse to the line using your outside calf. Don't let him cut corners.

You can also take a **bending line** over fences. This line is just like the arc of a circle. Generally, you take actual fences on a straight line and only use a bending line between jumps. It's really important to maintain an impulsive and balanced canter when riding a curve. Turning aids must be applied without slowing the tempo of the canter. Bending lines come into their own when you're riding against the clock. The competitor who rides the fastest and finds the shortest arcs between fences will get the fastest time.

Flex your horse inward when practicing a bending line.

Three exercises for riding a bending line:

1. Place a ground pole at the mid-point of a 20-meter circle. Ride the circle in all gaits, keeping the circle nice and rounded. Remember that you should also clear the pole on a bending line. Immediately after the pole, riders often forget to maintain bend, and the circle's third quarter becomes rather angular. Maintain an inward bend at all times, turning with the aid of your outside calf.

2. Build a fence in the center of the arena, along the centerline and facing the long sides. Jump it first on a circle, from both directions. Then ride a figure eight. You will change the circle and direction over the jump. Use a leading rein as you go over the fence and always look in the new direction. If your horse doesn't change canter lead at the fence, change it by trotting briefly after the fence. Remember to keep your curves rounded and symmetrical.

3. Also practice riding curves in between fences. Build two fences on either side of the centerline so that, seen from above, they form a letter V. The corner between the fences should be a right angle – 90 degrees – so they won't be in the way of each other. Jump the fences in turn on a large figure eight. Count the number of canter strides between fences. By how much are you able to shorten your arc? How many canter strides do you need to complete your loop?

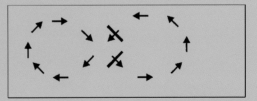

You're on a **diagonal** when you travel diagonally from one straight line to another. Going across the long diagonal is an example of a diagonal. Turn into a diagonal using a leading rein and your outside calf. When following a diagonal to the left, always look left. Move your left hand straight out to the left, leading slightly with the knuckle of your pinky finger. Be careful not to pull the rein backwards. Support the turn using your opposite calf, in this case the right one.

When a fence is built on a diagonal, you will normally change direction while going over it. You must therefore prepare to change canter lead over the fence. Usually it's enough to look in the new direction and use a leading rein. If you let your horse know the new direction fast enough, he'll automatically take the correct lead.

When a diagonal is located between two fences, it becomes a diagonal line. Look closely at fences 6 and 7 on the sample course pictured on page 72.

A leading rein will let your horse know that you wish to change direction – while still jumping a fence.

Tempo

Along with taking a good line to a fence, you also have to approach it at a suitable tempo. If you approach too slowly, your horse may stop in front of the fence and refuse to jump. And if you canter toward a fence too slowly, your horse will make a really powerful take-off and an angular jump. His jump arc will then be angular instead of rounded, and you'll be in danger of knocking down the back rail of a spread in particular. Too much speed can also cause problems. Can you be sure of steering your horse into the fence if he's charging toward it? If his speed is not controlled, your horse's jump arc will be flat, and you will be more likely to knock down the fence.

How do you gauge the best tempo for jumping a course? Each class at a show jumping competition will have a certain tempo assigned to it. It may be, for example, 985 feet per minute. If you're riding around a 66 ft x 132 ft arena, the track's circumference will be about 328 feet. You'd therefore ride around the school about three times in a minute. Naturally, you won't simply ride around a track when jumping a course – you'll also ride corners, curves and fences. Remember that you'll lose time if your horse refuses. You'll also gain faults if you exceed the time limit set for a course, so the correct speed is vital!

It's important to approach fences at the correct speed. Is the rider in this picture already going too fast?

You can practice tempo adjustments using related distances. For horses, the standard **related distances** for show jumps are as follows:
48 feet – 3 canter strides
60 feet – 4 canter strides
72 feet – 5 canter strides.

If you ride these distances at a slower tempo, you'll require more canter strides to cover the distance. Tempo therefore also refers to the length of a stride.

Ponies have naturally shorter canters than horses. So pony riders have a good reason to get to know their pony's canter and adjust it to fit the related distances. Ponies will usually take one extra canter stride over a certain distance than a horse will. Almost all competition courses will contain at least one related distance.

Balance and canter rhythm

In addition to everything we've previously mentioned, a successful jump requires a **balanced team of horse and rider** and a **suitable canter rhythm**. If horse and rider are to move together in balance, the

Practice adjusting tempo:

Place two ground poles to the inside of the track along the long side. Check that the poles are on a straight line and measure out a distance of 58 feet between them.

1. Canter over the poles normally and count how many strides you take between poles. Remember to keep a steady canter along the entire line. At first, you may find it hard to count your horse's strides when in the saddle. Ask a friend or your riding instructor to count the strides out loud. Be precise – don't count the strides taken going over the poles, just those between them.

2. Slow down your tempo and slightly shorten the canter. Try to take one more canter stride between poles.

3. Increase your tempo and lengthen the canter. Try to take one less canter stride between the poles than on your first attempt.

Did you manage to get five canter strides on your first attempt, six on your second, and four on your third? Repeat this exercise, but replace the poles with small fences.

rider's seat must be stable over fences and in between them. Practice your light seat in all gaits, including transitions and gridwork. You mustn't disturb your horse through your seat, even if he makes a bigger jump than expected.

When your seat is correct, you can focus on canter rhythm. You shouldn't be constantly pulling on the reins, nor continually urging your horse forward with your calves. When held back, a horse that's charging forwards wildly is no more in balance than one that's just trundling along! When riding at your best, you'll be able to apply your aids without disturbing the rhythm of the canter. You'll then be able to count a steady 1-2-3-1-2-3 rhythm all round the course. This will also help when deciding the correct moment to take off for a fence.

A seat and rhythm exercise
Place three single bars to the inside of the track along the long side. Measure out a distance of 8 feet between bars for ponies, and 10 feet for horses. Ride a working canter on a straight line over the single bars. Your horse will clear them with bounce jumps. There will be no canter strides between fences, just a sequence of small bounces one after the other. Maintain a light seat and light rein contact throughout the exercise. If your balance is good, you'll also be able to complete this exercise in a basic seat without stirrups, moving with the motion of the jumps.

A bounce combination of cross bars.

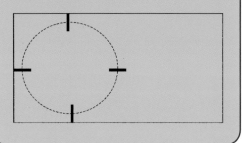
The take-off point

The **take-off point** also affects whether or not a jump is successful, because the apex of your horse's jump must coincide with the highest point of a fence. A good rule of thumb is that the best take-off point for a fence is located at a distance in front of the fence that is equal to the fence's height. A horse can, of course, jump from closer in or further away. It's far more important to aim for a good line and tempo on your approach than finding the perfect take-off point.

You can compare judging the take-off point to a baseball player having an eye for the ball. At what point do you have to swing the bat to hit the moving ball? Riders will be able to look at a fence and get a feel for whether they need to shorten or lengthen the canter to ensure that the final canter stride will result in a suitable take-off point. You must **train your eyes**. If you are to judge the correct take-off distance, you must keep your eye on the fence throughout your entire approach.

Moving with the motion of the jump

You must next learn to **move with the motion of the jump**. Rise into a light seat at take-off and relax your arms. When your horse rises into his jump, release the reins and use your upper body to balance your light seat. When you reach the apex of the jump, start looking at the next fence. As you come down from the jump, straighten your upper body and bring your hands gently back to take up rein contact. You'll now be able to steer your horse from the very first stride he takes after landing.

It's as easy as pie, right? In fact, not all jumps are the same, so you won't be able to avoid making mistakes or losing your balance. A classic mistake when moving with the motion of the jump is for riders to lean too far over the horses' manes with their upper bodies. They will then be slower to straighten up and balance

the canter after the jump. And if you lean too far into a jump, you may well end up with a noseful of mane! Another common mistake is not to move in time with the horse's jump. See what happens when the rider on page 66 "jumps before her pony." Here, the rider thought her pony was going to take off for a jump one canter stride before he actually did. She "jumped" too soon, and see how she ended up.

When jumping a course, always turn to look at the next fence while still jumping the previous one.

65

Practice moving with the motion of the jump

Build three small verticals to the inside of the track along the long side. Measure out a distance of 48 feet between fences. Ride a working canter on a straight line over the fences. You should take three canter strides between each fence. When you can canter over the fences straight and with your arms relaxed, start changing the height and appearance of the fences. Place a water tray under the middle fence. Raise the final fence. Change the first fence into a high-sided cross bar. When the jumps change, you'll have to change how you move to the new motion.

Moving with the motion of the jump can sometimes be tricky.

An excellent way to practice moving to the motion of the jump is by jumping a gymnastic line. Although gymnastic lines are combinations that you won't find at competitions, they make for highly beneficial exercises. They'll enhance horse and rider's balance, improve jumps, and help you learn to move with the motion of the jump. Build up gymnastic lines one element at a time. Don't add the next element until you've gotten the hang of the previous one. Adjust distances to suit your horse. The following example of a gymnastic line should be approached at a trot. Canter is taken up after the first cross bar, with one canter stride between subsequent fences.

An example of a gymnastic line:
trot pole – 10 feet
cross bar – 18-feet
vertical – 21-feet
– oxer

You can use gymnastic lines to practice moving with the motion of the jump.

It's worth practicing a trot approach, even though you'll usually approach fences at a canter. For trot approaches, you should place a ground pole in front of the fence. The ground pole helps your horse judge the correct take-off point. The pole should be placed about 8 - 10 feet in front of the fence. This distance will be shorter for ponies than for horses. All of your horse's legs should have stepped over the ground pole before take-off.

Note! The last fence in a gymnastic line may be slightly higher. The smaller obstacles leading into this fence will aid your approach to it. If the distances have been adjusted to your horse's movements, take-off will not occur too close to or too far away from the obstacles.

The horse's task

Even though the rider has plenty to do when taking a fence, it's always the horse that does the actual jumping. A broad definition of the rider's job is to guide both the movements between fences and the horse's jumps. In order for your horse to be able to jump, you'll have to learn to move with the motion of his jump without disturbing him. Your horse will naturally be able to control his own tempo, balance and rhythm. And what's best, he can judge the take-off distance for himself, too. A good jumper will react to your aids, while at the same time boldly making his own decisions about when to take off.

When your horse jumps, he first raises his forelegs and propels his whole body into the air using his hind legs. When jumping at his best, he will raise his knees high and tuck his forelegs tightly under him, near to his belly. His withers will be the highest point of his body during a round jump, as his head and neck will stretch forwards and down to balance the jump. His hind legs will stretch out far behind and will follow almost as an extension of his belly line. Your horse will land from a balanced jump in true canter, forelegs leading and hind legs following gently behind.

Jumping technique is largely a natural characteristic of each individual horse, and practice won't do much to alter it. If your horse has a habit of not lifting his knees and letting his forelegs hang over a jump, he may never change his ways. You can of course jump a horse like this, but you'll have to pay attention to his jumping style and the height of the fences you jump.

But fence height isn't the be-all and end-all. Show jumping isn't about who dares to jump the highest fence – it's a measure of the skills of both horse and rider and how they work together as a team. You should be prouder of completing a clean, balanced and faultless 28 inch course than putting in a dangerous-looking, unstable and rhythmless performance over a 3 feet 3 inch course. Only top-level horses will be able to jump 5 foot courses. The jumping capacity of your average horse will only be sufficient for courses up to about 3 feet 3 inches.

Over the course

Fences on a competition course will quickly follow one after the other and will put all your training to the test. Before a competition, it's worth doing exercises over single obstacles and short courses.

Every competition class has a different course and its own judging criteria, which will focus on faults or time. Most of them aim for both a fast

The jump arc from take-off to landing.

and faultless performance. Show jumping is choc full of excitement. Who will find the fastest track for the jump-off? Who will manage to clear a challenging combination cleanly? Will a brightly colored wall lead to surprise and refusals?

Horse and rider at a gate.

The oxers you'll find on a show jumping course will usually be parallels.

there won't be enough room to ride on a straight line before the obstacles. Straight lines, bending lines and diagonals are classed as natural. There must be room for a horse to take sufficient strides both before and after a fence, even though you may want to choose a slightly more challenging and faster line to win a jump-off.

The course designer will draw up the course plan for a competition. Fences will be placed on very different lines. Course plans will not usually have lines drawn on them to show a mandatory track – competitors may choose their own. Fences cannot be placed where they would require an "unnatural" line. For example, combinations cannot be built along the short side of a small arena, because

You need skill to design and draw a course plan. Like maps, course plans must be drawn to scale. One inch on paper can stand for ten feet in real life. If the length of the long side is 130 feet, you won't be able to fit more than one combination or related line along it easily.

Even this triple bar is cleared with speed on a course.

It's vital to maintain a steady rhythm and tempo over the entire course. When you avoid unnecessary movements, you'll be better able to judge correct take-off distances. A balanced jump arc will also make it easier to move with the motion of the jump. Ideally, you'll ride the whole course in a balanced canter and be able to count a steady 1-2-3-1-2-3 rhythm. You can practice a steady rhythm and tempo by doing jumping exercises at one end of the school and exercises to improve your aids at the other.

An exercise to help you improve your aids and maintain a steady tempo and rhythm:

Place 5 single bars along the long side with a distance of 12 feet between each bar. The bars should be cleared as a bounce exercise – there should be no canter strides between them. Remember, it's your job to control your horse's canter strides using your calf and rein aids. When you find a suitable rhythm and tempo for this exercise, maintain it for the following jumping exercise. If you lose the rhythm at any time, return to this exercise.

You can build two related distances as a jumping exercise – one on a straight line and one on a curved line. Take a look at fences 1, 2, 3 and 4 on the sample course plan. If you build them all as verticals, you can jump them from both directions.

You can set up the aid improvement exercise in place of the combination (5a and 5b).

A sample of a practice course plan:

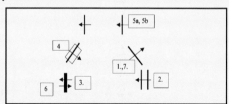

1. Approach fence number one on a diagonal. First ride around the track. Use a left leading rein to steer onto the line for the fence. Start turning right over the fence – use a right leading rein while still in the air to ensure that you land in true canter. It's worth starting out with a trot approach to this fence. Replace the vertical with a cross bar and place a trot pole about 9 feet in front of it.

2.–3. A straight related distance. 72 feet = 5 canter strides. Is your horse used to walls? Fence number three is a wall.

4. A water tray beneath a fence requires a careful line. You must also ride the horse forward in a forceful yet controlled canter. And once again you'll change canter lead, this time from right to left.

5. Precision over the combination! Remember to adjust the distance to both the height of the fences and your horse's stride. Check the tips in the section titled Combinations.

6.–7. A related distance on a diagonal line. 72 feet = 5 canter strides. Use a leading rein between fences to get on line for the final fence. Remember that you must never just stop riding as soon as you've cleared the last fence. After the seventh fence, change canter lead again, picking up a right lead and maintaining a steady tempo and rhythm.

Such a short course and yet so much to do! And at a competition, you'll have to do it all in a single round and in just a few crazy minutes. So you'll need practice, practice and more practice. First complete the elements of the course as single fences, starting with the easier ones. Only jump the course as a whole once you can complete all the single fences without fault. Don't get upset if you don't immediately manage to jump every obstacle to the best of your ability. Keep practicing those sections that aren't going too well. And keep in mind that practice makes champions!

Tips for building fences:

- When practicing, you can place a ground pole about 4 inches in front of a jump. A clear ground line will enable your horse to get a better feel for the fence.
- Start by building single obstacles and courses using only poles, as they're easier to move around than entire fences.
- On a course plan, a single line denotes a vertical, two lines an oxer, and three lines a triple bar.
- Remember that horses have a strong herd instinct: a difficult fence is worth jumping toward the stable or other horses.

4. Cross-country

Cross-country is part of eventing, which tests both horse and rider's skills in dressage, show jumping and endurance. The endurance test includes a cross-country section that requires speed, courage and strength from both horse and rider. It is the "soul" of eventing.

Cross-county fences differ from show jumping fences in two main ways. Firstly, there is no arena railing or wall surrounding them. Secondly, there are no dislodgeable elements – all fences are **solid**.

A solid fence may sound quite daunting. What if your horse's jump is too flat? That can, of course, happen, but your horse's legs will usually just slide over the fence with a few minor knocks. It's rare for a horse to get stuck across a correctly built fence. The upside of solid fences is that a falling pole won't roll around your horse's legs.

Long, thick, smooth **tree trunks** make for excellent and safe cross-country fences. You can provide extra support to keep them in place by sinking standards into the ground on either side. The fence must remain firmly in place and should not wobble if knocked by a horse's legs.

Solid cross-country fences on grass.

You ride much more quickly over a cross-country course than you do over show jumps – and you'll have to clear fences going both up and downhill. Does that sound crazy? Cross-country riding isn't for the faint-hearted, and you always have to focus on safety. However, for many, a successfully cleared cross-country course is such a magnificent experience that these calculated risks are worth taking. Practice cross-country fences with a competent instructor who will be able to advise you on how to complete your exercises safely.

A log fence is a wonderfully easy cross-country obstacle to set up.

Types of cross-country obstacles

Some types of cross-country obstacles are similar to those found in show jumping – verticals, oxers and triple bars. They're just made from slightly different materials. A vertical may consist of logs about the thickness of your arm piled one atop the other. Or it could look like a country gate. Most cross-country jumps are, however, reminiscent of spreads. Thinner and fatter logs may be placed one after the other so that, from the side, they clearly look like an ascending oxer.

The positioning of a cross-country fence also plays a major role. When a fence has to be jumped going up or downhill, you'll need extra care and skill to clear it. Cross-

Never jump cross-country fences without a safety helmet and safety vest!

country fences don't have any dislodgeable elements, so you can't gain faults for knocking them down. Run outs, refusals, exceeding the optimum time, or sliding out of the saddle will, however, still send you dropping down in the ranking.

Fences on flat terrain

If a fence is located on flat terrain, the type and appearance of the fence will dictate how challenging it is to jump. Easy fences are wide and low and can be cleared on a straight line. Fences may also be located on a bending line or on a corner. Narrow fences are challenging, because you must be able to steer your horse into them at a brisk canter. Fences may also be asymmetrical. An oxer that, when seen from above, looks like a triangle makes for a far longer jump on one side than on the other. But then again, how do you make sure your horse jumps over the narrow section without running out?

A stack of old telephone poles makes a fine cross-country vertical.

Although this fence is located on flat terrain, it's still challenging. The side with the brush requires a much longer jump than the side with the flag.

76

You'll also find cross-country combinations. Show jumping combinations contain a maximum of three elements, but a cross-country combination may have more. And a cross-country combination doesn't even have to be on a straight line. These kinds of technical obstacles are challenging, but they help separate the wheat from the chaff. It's not enough to ride your horse boldly forward at a brisk tempo – you have to ride an exceptionally precise line to each fence to meet the challenge with flying colors.

Unlike in show jumping, if your horse refuses one fence in a combination, you don't have to start again from element A. Element A may involve jumping onto a bank, element B a jump atop the bank, and element C a jump down from the bank. If your horse refuses the bank down, you can try element C again without having to go back to element A.

Uphill and downhill fences

The character of a standard cross-country fence changes dramatically when you place it on uphill or downhill terrain. You'll need to be extremely well balanced as you approach a downhill fence. Take special care to ensure that your horse is not traveling on the forehand. Use plenty of half-halts and don't lean too far forward. When you take off from above a fence, your horse will not need to jump very high. An experienced eventer will jump low to ensure a soft landing. Although a fence may only be 2 feet high when you take off, the drop during landing may be as much as 3 feet 3 inches. Maintain light rein contact during the landing and keep your weight in the stirrups. Make sure that your upper body does not lean forward.

An inexperienced eventer may be a little too enthusiastic in his take-off. Be careful when landing!

Taking off uphill for a tire fence.

the bank down. The bank down will correspond to the landing phase. Shift your weight into the stirrups, look ahead, and relax your arms into the release. Make sure that your upper body remains straight and that you don't destabilize the bank down by pushing your horse onto the forehand.

It's important to find a good take-off point when jumping an uphill fence. The farther away your horse's take-off point is, the higher he will have to jump. The height of a fence on a slope is measured from its probable take-off point. If an uphill fence is 2 feet 9 inches high and your horse takes off about 8 inches below it, you'll need enough height to clear a 3 foot 3 inch fence. Approach an uphill fence in a strong, assertive canter.

Steps up and down

A **bank** is a cross-country obstacle that involves jumping onto the obstacle. The first take-off is merely for the bank up. The horse simply jumps up onto the bank and there is no landing phase. Your task is to move with the motion of the take-off and bank up, so rise into a light seat and release the reins. When your horse has jumped onto the bank, start preparing for

Cross-country obstacles may incorporate a variety of steps that require only the up or down part of a jump. Ride a step up vigorously, but stay in control. The landing phase will be missing, so be prepared for the jump to stop mid-way. Steps down demand precision and should be ridden at a moderate tempo. Ensure that your horse moves immediately forward after landing. If you lose speed during a step down, the landing can cause a big jolt through the saddle.

Coffins

Coffins sound pretty creepy, but really a coffin is just a ditch you have to jump over. This obstacle can involve just a coffin, or the coffin can be placed below a fence. The edges of a coffin should be clearly marked so that horses can distinguish it from the surrounding terrain. For some horses, clearing a coffin is just another little leap, while others regard

A bank up.

A dry coffin

Start practicing dry coffins using a tarp placed between poles. The tarp is darker than the ground. To a horse, this will look like a deep pit. You can therefore practice coffins without the need for a shovel.

Look directly forward during a bank down to ensure that you'll continue smoothly forward after landing.

You can build this kind of practice dry coffin without digging a hole.

them with extreme caution. A timid horse may suddenly put on the brakes when approaching a coffin. If such a horse does decide to be bold and take the coffin, he may jump too high into the air. Practice jumping coffins and gradually get your horse accustomed to them.

Water

Water is an important element in cross-country obstacles. Getting your horse used to moving through water must be done calmly and you must listen to your horse at all times. Wild horses will not generally go into the water willingly or for fun. That's why a horse that gets his hooves wet shows real trust in his rider. Your horse can never know how deep a strange pool of water is. There might be something ferocious in there, like a crocodile. Some horses soon get used to water, and may even come to enjoy wading and splashing around. Others will forever remain afraid of water. But when asked, a horse that trusts his rider will go into the kinds of places that he is naturally wary of.

Water is jumped cleanly in show jumping. You'll gain faults for a damp hoof. Things are quite different in cross-county – clearing a water obstacle means getting wet. In easy classes, this may simply mean cantering through a shallow puddle, while in higher classes, you may have to leap into the water as part of a high bank down. Fences can even be located in the water. Begin practicing for water obstacles by walking calmly into the water and back out again. Later, you can also trot and canter in the water. After that, it's time to add fences on the water's edge, and finally in the water itself.

Your horse will not be able to canter as fast in the water as he can on dry land. Be particularly careful when cantering in the water in case the drag unseats you. Try running at full speed into the water without falling! When jumping a fence from the water, splashes can also impair visibility and both horse and rider's ability to judge distance.

In high-level classes, it can be a long way down to the water.

You can't avoid splashes when you canter through water.

5. Trail riding skill tasks

Trail riding skill tasks refer to outdoor obstacles that don't require jumping. These include many things that will be familiar to you from trail rides. You'll come across similar tasks in Western riding – trail riding skill tasks form part of a Western horse's everyday life. A Western horse won't be spooked by ditches, bridges or traffic when you take him out to check the pastures or on a cattle drive. These days, saddle horses are mainly ridden in indoor and outdoor arenas. But they enjoy and need trail rides to ensure a sufficiently varied exercise regime.

Varied terrain and diverse skill tasks will improve your horse's balance and coordination. Building muscle condition over hilly ground is both fun and effective. Simply staring at the arena walls has to be depressing for a horse. That's why when horses finally get out on the trail, they may be so enthusiastic that they seem impossible to control. If you first practice your trail riding skills close to the stable yard, you'll find that you'll manage far better on an actual trail ride. Trail riding skill tasks will help you get your horse listening to your aids out on the trail, too.

You need trail riding skills to get over ditches and banks.

> You're bound to find natural trail riding skill tasks along your own trails. Once you've gotten permission from the landowner, you can also build extra tasks along your route.

Even though trail riding skill tasks don't involve any jumping, you shouldn't underestimate them. Riding over varied terrain, opening gates from horseback, and other tricky tasks really do put a horse and rider's teamwork skills to the test. You may be surprised by how many different trail riding skill tasks there are – and how fun they are! Think about the kinds of situations you could come across out on the trail. Has a spring flood covered part of the trail? Can you lead your horse up a steep slope? How does your horse react to dog walkers strolling through the forest? Think up exercises for such situations and practice them in advance, somewhere close to the stable yard.

Different terrain

A **sandy trail** makes for firm yet yielding going, and riding along these trails is a superb way to relax. And if the terrain is flat and free of traffic, you can also ride at a faster pace. If you're in control of your horse, there's nothing to stop you from a little cantering.

It's also pleasant to ride on **grass**, but be careful if it's rained recently, as damp grass may be super slippery.

You must be particularly careful over **stony ground**. Give your horse enough rein so that he can turn his head and look for suitable places between the rocks for his hooves. Remember that there must be some flat spaces between the rocks where your horse can step. It's not worth riding over ground that's nothing but sharp stones and large expanses of rock.

> Check your horse's hooves after you return from a trail ride. Stones the size of your thumb can easily get stuck in the frog cleft and press uncomfortably against the sole of the hoof.

It's great to ride along sandy trails.

Never travel faster than a walk when on **asphalt**. Trotting and cantering on hard surfaces will put strain on your horse's joints. Besides, motorized vehicles will no doubt be traveling along such roads. Let your horse get used to cars and motorcycles in calm surroundings, such as at the stables or in other safe yards.

White crosswalks painted onto dark asphalt can startle many horses. Maybe they imagine them to be zebras, and want to walk around their relatives? In fact, horses see colors and depth in a different way than humans. To a horse, the dark spaces between the white lines may appear to be deep and uncrossable shafts.

Some **bridges and duckboards** (wooden planking) are true trail riding skill tasks. The clunk of your horse's hooves over a wooden bridge will sound very different from the noise they make over soft sand. It takes real care and trust to get your horse to walk along narrow planks. Always check beforehand that the structure can bear your combined weight without tilting. Bridges and duckboards designed for humans may not necessarily carry the weight of a horse. Equine duckboards are built with horses in mind, and are much wider than those built for humans.

Your horse's hooves will clunk on the wooden planks of equine duckboards.

A bridge may also be higher than the surrounding terrain. When faced with an obstacle like this that needs to be climbed, make sure your horse steps up onto the bridge rather than simply trying to jump over it.

You can build a variety of surfaces using **different colored tarps** and **thick fabrics.** Blue cloth can look like a puddle of water to your pony. Whose horse will dare to walk over a rustling tarp without changing pace or getting spooked? These kinds of tasks promote teamwork between horse and rider and will teach you a lot

A thin crust of ice on the surface of a puddle won't bother a bold pony.

Even a dry ditch can be challenging to cross. Although Pauli could have easily walked this ditch, he decided to treat his rider to a little jumping action.

about your horse's reactions. Cover the edges of fabric with a thick layer of sand or gravel so they don't get puckered up and tangled around your horse's legs. And don't go over fabrics or tarps if your horse is wearing studded shoes! The studs will ruin your "terrain" and may get caught in a tarp.

Water, an element familiar from cross-country obstacles, is also a challenging surface for trail riding skill tasks. Will your horse try to avoid puddles? The first time, try to steer your horse through the only puddle on the track. If your horse is truly on your aids, he'll step into it, even if he'd rather feel dry earth beneath his hooves. And what about when an overnight frost has frozen the surface of a puddle? Will your horse dare to be an icebreaker?

Uphill and downhill slopes

Riding up and downhill will improve both your and your horse's balance. Battling uphill also provides a great way of keeping fit. The steeper the slope, the more careful you'll have to be with regard to the terrain. Hilly ground needs to be firm and solid. A slippery hill is dangerous, as are banks with loose gravel or sand that will slide beneath your horse's hooves.

Rise into a light seat when going uphill. Your horse will stretch out his neck as he climbs, so be sure to follow his movements with your hands. When climbing a really steep slope, you can lean fairly far forward and hold onto the mane. Make sure to maintain a light rein contact in case your horse decides to charge off and bound up the hill like a jackrabbit.

Riding downhill is also challenging. Most of your horse's weight will shift onto his forelegs and his hind legs will thrust forward under his belly to maintain his balance. Shift your weight into the stirrups and relax your arms. Maintain light rein contact, so that you can put on the brakes or provide support with the reins if necessary. Don't lean forward – your task is to make sure that your own weight does not add to the load your horse is already carrying on his forelegs. When faced with a really steep downhill slope, it would be wise to find another route, or at least dismount and lead your horse down.

Remember to practice leading your horse! If you have to dismount for a steep downhill slope, your horse should not ride roughshod over you, even though he's following behind.

Your horse must be strong to climb a steep slope.

Always maintain a calm walk when going downhill.

Riding under a tarp is a fun exercise to improve trust and cooperation. You should build up to this in stages so that you don't spook your horse too much. Tie a rope tightly between two trees. You'll need help, as you'll have to set the rope at least 10 feet above the ground. Hang a blanket or tarp on the rope, just as if you were hanging out laundry on a clothesline. When you ride under the tarp the first time, make sure that it doesn't touch your horse. Only the button of your riding helmet is allowed to brush the tarp. If your horse trusts you throughout this exercise, you can try lowering the tarp. Your horse will eventually learn to "dive" under the tarp, while you lie down across his mane and listen to the tarp rustling at your back.

Gates

Opening different types of gates from horseback is an excellent teamwork exercise. You'll need plenty of time and patience at first, as you'll have to open the gate with one hand while you steer your horse with the other. This is where your dressage skills will come in handy, as you should be able to stop, leg yield, and ride a turn on the forehand or haunches.

Opening and closing gates from horseback requires patience.

Tie a thick rope to the arena gate. Try opening and closing it from horseback – can you manage it without dropping the end of the rope?

Other trail users

Who else will you meet out on the trail? Joggers, dog walkers, or berry pickers? In the winter, you might even bump into skiers or snowmobiles. The more familiar and safer your route is, the more startling it will be for your horse to encounter strangers. Horses love routine and always get stressed when their routines are broken. A sensitive horse may practically die of fright when she sees a familiar person from the stables picking berries. Not only is this person in the wrong place, but also in a weird, squatting position. Greet everyone you meet in a friendly manner. When your horse senses that you are calm and hears them speaking like "normal" people, she'll calm down.

Get your horse accustomed to meeting a variety of people and animals in the safety of the stable yard. Ask your friends to act as skiers, berry pickers, dog walkers, and joggers. Ride around the arena talking to the people you "meet." You're sure to have a good laugh as you all get into your roles! If your actors are also horse lovers, they'll know to tone down the swinging of their ski poles if your horse is clearly getting spooked. And if this scary skier also digs out a tasty treat from her pocket, your horse will have an extra reason to make friends with these monsters in the future.

It's also a good idea to introduce your horse to motorized vehicles in careful stages. A horseperson with a car will be the best help. Find a safe stretch of road in or near the stable yard to practice on. First ride past a stationary car. Ask the driver to open the window and talk to you as you pass the vehicle. The next stage is

Country paths are home to many sports and pastimes. Always pass anyone you meet at a walk.

A trained tarp "diver" will know to keep his muzzle down before going in.

It's a good idea to get your horse used to passing vehicles in the safety of the stable yard.

to have the engine running, but keep the vehicle stationary. If your horse remains confident, the car can drive toward you from the opposite direction. A vehicle approaching from behind is usually the most frightening, so only attempt this once the other stages are going really well. When automobiles are a familiar concept, you can try the same with mopeds, motorcycles, and snowmobiles.

Winning shouldn't be the be-all and end-all in competitions. Your goal is to enhance the trust and teamwork between you and your horse. When a skilled horsewoman trains diligently with her horse, they'll get wonderful results over any obstacle!

Why not design a trail riding skills course for you and your friends and hold a fun competition? The judge can award 0-10 points for each task. Here's a sample course:

1. crossing a tarp in the arena
2. opening and closing a gate
3. crossing a ditch
4. passing a stationary vehicle with its engine running
5. riding uphill onto a knoll
6. riding downhill from a knoll
7. pass a flapping clothesline
8. a forest "slalom" between marked trees
9. crossing through a puddle of water
10. crossing a wooden bridge

6. Hints and tips from famous European riders

Interviews by Pernilla Linder

Maria Gretzer

Who is Maria Gretzer?

She is the girl in town who has always loved animals – horses in particular. She got her parents to let her take lessons at a riding school. She rode once a week even though she was so nervous she could hardly sleep the night before.

And though her parents initially thought that she would grow tired of horses, she never did.

Maria was finally allowed to lease a pony for a year.

Eventually, she got a horse of her own: not a good beginner's horse, but an old Thoroughbred racing horse who wasn't very expensive – and wasn't exactly healthy, either.

"That horse was ill or lame almost the entire first year I had it," Maria recalls.

But Maria still didn't give up - in fact she did just the opposite.

She kept going.

"You can't take less care of a horse just because it's sick," she says. "It needs at least as much care as any other, and usually even more."

Maria's a real horse person. And a real pro!

In fact, she had all the qualities needed to make it to the very top.

She says she's not that talented a rider, but it's not true. Maria's just humble.

Maria may be one of the very best show jumpers (and riders in general!) in the entire world.

She's won hundreds of competitions in her home country of Sweden and abroad, on many different horses – including a horse she bred herself named Movie Star, a stallion named Feliciano, a big white mare named Marcoville, and, most recently, Feliciano's son, a stallion named Hip Hop.

But Maria didn't exactly get everything handed to her on a silver platter.

She didn't grow up in a family that liked horses, with horsey parents who had their own stable, who considered riding and competing a natural part of everyday life.

Far from it.

"My parents have always been sensible and understanding," she says. "They've always supported me. But they weren't horse people at all, so I had to gain knowledge and experience by myself."

And did she ever!

Maria went abroad, first to Germany. She worked in stables, far from the glamorous life. She was up at six every morning: cleaning stables from top to bottom; grooming, saddling and bridling horses; and taking care of their every need. After a while, she was allowed to ride the horses, and eventually, she started competing.

She was talented, careful, and ambitious; a dream combination for any horse owner.

After Germany, Maria moved to Switzerland. There she worked for the famous show jumper and trainer Paul Weier, and she became more and more interested in eventing, with its versatility, speed and excitement.

"I definitely think you shouldn't specialize in anything too early," she says. "The most important thing is for you to get the basics down."

After six years working with horses abroad, Maria felt ready to come home again.

Her parents bought a beautiful old farm in Skåne, in southern Sweden, and her whole family moved there. The dream of a real horse life had become reality!

And then came the success.
Maria's methodical groundwork paid off.

She took on more difficult jumping and became an elite show jumper. Next she accepted a spot on the Swedish national team, where she competed in national championships. European championships, world championships, and the Olympics followed ...

And today, she's Sweden's show jumping national team manager. All of the top riders want her there, and Maria knows exactly what each rider wants and needs, of course. She knows almost everyone in the international show jumping circles, and she's a sensible, good leader who can get everyone to do their best and work together as a team.

So you can trust that when Maria gives you her best advice, as she's giving you super tips from a super pro.

Here's what she has to say:

On riding at a riding school:
"It's always good to start riding at a riding school, I think," Maria says. "A good riding school is a great environment in which to begin. The school community, the classes, all the friends – you'd miss all that otherwise. I think it's a given that you should ride for your first few years at a good riding school. It's almost impossible to start off with your own horse and get the basics down well."

At a riding school, there's also a better chance of getting good teachers.

"You shouldn't have an elite trainer from the start," Maria says. "You should have a trainer who's good at teaching you the basics; someone who can get results through play and make riding really, really fun."

About your first horse:
After a few years at a riding school it's a good idea, and lots of fun, to make the next step of owning a horse or pony, Maria says.

"But the first horse or pony should be experienced! It should be a real teacher for you!"

"Your first horse can definitely be a little older. It has to be healthy, of course – that's important – but it's good to find a horse whose been 'puttering around' for a few years, doing some easy jumping."

"It should definitely be a horse that's reliable and not easy to scare. It should be able to handle a rider who makes mistakes."

The first horse or pony should be able to show the rider the ropes, Maria points out, very sensibly:

"I think a good horse is the best teacher and trainer you can ever have," she says. "If you don't have a good horse, then it doesn't matter what elite trainer you have. There is no better way to learn than to experience the horse doing the right thing – when you 'push the right buttons'!"

About equipment:
It's good to buy some important things new, Maria thinks. It's a reasonable investment. For other things, you can definitely buy used items.

"A helmet and safety vest – those are things I think you should buy new so they are reliable," she says. "With an old helmet, for example, you never know. It might've been through a fall, making it much less safe than it once was."

Gear for the horse, such as a saddle, can be bought used. It can even be to your advantage to have a saddle that is "broken in" when you get it.

"Just make sure that everything fits and, of course, that the leather is whole and in good condition, before you buy anything second-hand," Maria points out.

You probably don't need as many things as you think you do.

Sometimes, you can go nuts buying too much equipment, Maria thinks.

"There really aren't many horses that need breast plates, four leggings, extra saddle pads and so on," she says.

"Don't throw money away on a lot of unnecessary stuff – and definitely don't buy equipment and put it on your horse if you don't even know what it's called!"

"I use a bridle, saddle and leggings on the forelegs. I usually don't use anything else on my horses."

About warming up before riding:

"The warm-up is really important," Maria says. "It's important to understand that the horse has to be limber before you can do anything with it."

You should warm up by walking for about ten minutes. Then you can jog, either trotting or cantering, straight ahead, without demanding anything special of the horse.

"You definitely shouldn't demand anything at this stage. The horse should feel that this is nothing but a warm-up. Then you pause for a while, and then the actual work starts!"

The horse will also learn that the warm-up is serious. Work, and then a reward afterwards!

"I think the most important part is finding a good rhythm in your riding," Maria says. "Your pony shouldn't run, but it shouldn't drag its legs either. You should find a good, easy rhythm. The pony should be attentive and listen to you."

About preparing for competitions:

Maria's best tip is to make sure to arrive early for competitions.

"That's really important," she says. "Make sure you're prepared, have everything packed, and have your horse and tack organized. And make sure to take everything you'll need!"

"It's awful to have to run around in a hurry to finish paperwork, walk the course and everything. It's much better to be early. Then you have the time to sit down for a while and think everything through, and take plenty of time to walk the course."

"And it's never wrong to warm up for a little longer than usual. I think it's much better to walk a little longer during show warm-ups. The horse calms down, relaxes. And that goes for you too!"

About walking the course:

Make it a good habit to walk the course carefully, Maria says.

"It's also good to walk with your trainer or someone who can help. But I think you should do it alone at least once or twice. Then you can really focus."

It's not good, according to Maria, to do this with your friends.

"We all know how easy it is to lose focus. You end up talking about other things instead."

"Because remember," she says, "that when you enter the course with your pony, everything moves much, much quicker! You need to make sure you know where to go to be able to do well!"

Pernilla Linder Velander

A practice tip from Maria:
My tip is to not specialize when you're young!

In the beginning, you should try to get the basics down well. You should get a kind of all-around education in your riding. Ride some cross-country, compete in dressage as well as jumping. Practice tempo riding or racing – do everything! This will give you a sound base, if you later – hopefully – want to get deeper into show jumping!

And one more thing – try to always have someone with you when you're jumping. You should never jump by yourself. Always have someone with you who can help. It's safer, more convenient – and more fun!
Good luck!

Franke Sloothaak

"Your pony time should be a time for joy and playfulness!" Franke Sloothaak says.

"You have to have fun with your pony! Go out and play – make some mischief! Ride around with your friends – have some fun, too! Of course there has to be structure and work – but first of all, you should have fun with your horse!"

Franke knows, because that was how he started, when he was a very young boy in Holland.

"We rode out bareback," he says. "We got on our ponies and rode around with just a bridle. Everything was for fun, and there were no worries. We had fun with our ponies, and we learned a lot of stuff, almost without even noticing."

So, get up on your horse and just go!

Play catch, play cowboys and Indians, race over to that big tree and back again. Many riders will recognize these forms of play.

There has to be a pattern of fun from the beginning, you know.

"The more fun memories you have of your early pony rides," Franke says, "the better the chance that riding and horses are something you can't live without later in life."

And we certainly think he's right!

To Franke – and to many other pony riders –there's one more thing that's very important, right from the start, which is competition.

Franke started early with riding competitions, too. He was ten when he started at a riding school and had the chance to practice seriously.

It didn't take long for people to notice that he was very good, and a very talented rider. And believe it or not, after four years, when Franke was 14, he got to ride in his first European championship.

"I was chosen for the Dutch Junior team," he explains. "We went to Ireland to ride the championship. It was Henk Noren, Emile Hendrix, Rob Ehrens and me."

Every one of them is now a European riding star, and the team did very well. Franke and his team came home with the team silver medal, in their first championship.

There were to be many more championships for Franke.

The really big victories came after he moved from Holland to Germany. And he rode straight into the German national team, too.

Do you want to hear about his unbelievable accomplishments?

• Franke Sloothaak has ridden in four Olympic games. He has two Olympic gold medals with the German team.

• He has been the World Champion in jumping twice.

• At the world championship in The Hague, Netherlands 1994, he won both individually and with his team – and he won in his home country! Four years later he won the gold medal again in Rome.

• He has ridden the World Cup finals in show jumping 14 (!) times. Once he came in second, and twice he made it to third place.

• He has three gold medals, seven silvers and three bronzes in the German championships.

• Not to mention all the hundreds of victories and garlands he has collected in Grand Prix and difficult jumping all over the world.

Not too bad for the kid who started out by running around with a bridle in the pen on those mischievous ponies, right?

But Franke changed from ponies to big horses pretty quickly.

After only two years in his riding school he got to ride a small Arab. It was like a pony – quick, fast, and pretty fiery – but it was 59 inches high, so it competed against big horses.

"It was named Im-el-Loulou," Franke remembers. "And we rode a pretty big three-day event in Holland – and I became Leading Rider of the Show – the best rider in the entire competition!"

And then his career just took off.

When he was 16 Franke became the Dutch Junior master for the first time.

He got to ride different horses all the time.

As Franke and his horses won more victories, prospective buyers started to come and look at his promising horses.

"And in that situation, my parents couldn't keep them," Franke remembers.

"This of course felt sad. But there was a silver lining, too. It's a good thing to ride many different horses. You learn a lot. And I really wanted to learn! To develop, to become a better rider," he says.

His next big career break came about a year later. Franke got the chance to ride in a clinic for the famous jumper and trainer Alwin Schokemöhle. Schokemöhle discovered what a talent the tall Dutchman was.

"He asked me if I wanted to come stay with him and ride his horses," Franke remembers.

What a chance!

Franke accepted. He moved to Schokemöhle's big professional arena in Germany – and his successes just kept coming.

Franke got unbelievably great horses – and he rode them all wisely and equally well.

But nobody should think that life with horses is just one big party.

No rider can count on having only success and happiness. There's a lot of work to be done before you can ride in the big arenas, ride faultlessly, and be the fastest rider in a jump-off.

You need to use your head a little, too. If you're going to be the best rider in the arena, it helps to be very smart.

Franke tells us about something that really made him think:

"It was 1985, at a contest in Rotterdam, Holland," he remembers. "My horse fell on the course. I was thrown off, pretty badly, and my knee was injured. It took three or four months until I could even sit on a horse again."

"Those months gave me perspective. When something happens, you have to sort of stop and think. You get the time to analyze what you can do better."

"I'm sure that accident made me a better rider. And one thing is for sure – there's no doubt that it was the horses that motivated me to practice and come back again!"

"There are many things that can make you a successful rider," he says.

Of course, talent and feeling as a rider are crucial. You have to really love horses, really want to work with them. You have to practice and you have to ride good horses.

But there are certain personality traits that are almost as important, the champion Franke feels:

"There's this will to fight, to come back again, even when things are rough," he says. "You have to have self-discipline. You also must be open, and be able to take good advice.

"And you have to dare to believe in yourself!"

Franke's advice:

About ponies, when you're young:

Franke's own pony days didn't last very long. He got very tall and thin at an early age. It was obvious that he needed to move on to a big horse.

"And I think that's important," he says. "You shouldn't keep riding a pony if you're getting too tall. Today many kids are getting quite tall, even reaching six feet at an early age."

"If that's the case, it's important to switch to a horse," he says.

If you wait too long, the change will just be harder. It might almost feel like starting from scratch when you leave your pony and start riding a horse.

"So have fun with your pony," Franke says. "Enjoy all the fun and crazy stuff that happens during your pony time. Treasure it for as long you can."

"But don't wait too long before changing to a big horse. And try, if possible, to make your first big horse be a 'little' big one – as long as it's okay in other respects. Ideally, your first horse should also be a little experienced. And smart."

About the basics, and a correct position:

"Whenever you start," he says, "no matter how young or old you are: The most important thing of all is to get the basics down correctly!"

You need to learn to control all movements – the

horse's movements, and your own!

You need to practice finding and keeping your balance!

You have to be able to follow the horse, but also to be still and firm in the saddle – no matter what (almost!) your horse or pony does.

And how can you become a well-balanced expert?

"Ride A LOT without stirrups," Franke says.

"Practice sitting in the saddle and hugging the horse with your legs. Then you'll learn to sit in a way that's both efficient and flexible."

"I really want to give you a warning about one thing," he says. "You often see riders whose seats aren't quite steady and firm. And they then choose the easy way out and shorten their stirrups more and more."

"That's a trick that won't fool anybody but yourself," Franke says. "It's easy to stand up on your horse – if the horse is just moving forward."

"But when you're in a situation where you have to be able to drive – you'll notice that it won't work if you aren't balanced and have your horse 'on your legs'!"

About equipment:

First of all, you need good equipment to be able to sit correctly in the saddle – and therefore be able to influence your pony or horse in the right way.

The saddle has to be well placed on the horse. It also has to fit you as a rider, helping you to find a correct position in a natural way.

"And once again: If you don't sit correctly – you won't have a good influence on your horse!" Franke says.

"It's also important to use the correct headstall and bridle with a pony," he continues.

"I think it may be safer and better to use a bit that is a little sharper for a pony that's very temperamental," he says. "With a bit like that, the rider can ride much softer, have much softer hands, and leave more room for the horse – than if the rider has to pull on the reins all the time."

But with a sharp bit, of course you must never pull hard on your reins.

The bit that's a little sharper is used so you don't have to pull hard at the horse's mouth – and you can still be in control and ride safely.

Some more good advice:

Never experiment with different sharp bits on your own!

Only test new bits after consulting with your trainer, or with somebody else who is experienced and knowledgeable!

For the same reason – albeit inverted – it might be smart to ride with spurs, if your pony is a little on the slow and lazy side. In general, however, spurs are not for beginners.

"It's better to ride softly and gently with careful spurs to heighten your leg aids, than to sit and kick at your pony's sides," Franke feels. "That will only ruin your seat and your influence on the pony."

But of course you have to be a very good rider yourself, to be sure that you are using the spurs softly and gently.

Good luck!

Pernilla Linder Velander

Eventing is probably the toughest riding there is, and if you're going to compete at the top level, a lot of things have to be just right.

Your horse has to be well trained, brave and smart. It has to walk the dressage with a proper attitude, it has to be able to gallop cross-country like crazy – and it has to be able to show-jump very big obstacles.

And you, as a rider – well, you have to be at least as brave and smart as your horse.

You also have to be stubborn, unafraid and goal-conscious. And you really have to be a super horse person.

In other words, you have to be just like Piia Pantsu from Finland!

Piia is one of those super horse people. She loves horses. She has loved horses since she was seven, went to the stable with a friend for the first time – and fell in love with the horsey atmosphere.

Since then horses have virtually been her life. Eventing became her sport, because it's so cool to be able to do everything with your horse: all phases, from dressage to cross-country to show jumping.

Piia is a champion – having won the championships in Finland and Sweden. She rode in the European championship, took medals in several world championships, and rode in the Olympic games.   And yes, she won a silver medal in the world's hardest eventing competition, in Badminton, England (she was just a couple hundredths of a second off the winning time).

Piia and her husband Fredrik Jönsson, who are both Olympic riders in eventing, also compete in jumping.

"Well, you want to learn new things," Piia says. "And try to reach higher. I think eventing is the most fun of all, because you have to be totally well rounded. But then I wanted to move on and start specializing."

"I wanted to become a better rider, as well as a better horse teacher and trainer!" Piia says.

A really good rider is humble. She or he knows that there is always more to learn. Everybody can always become better.

Push on, and clench your teeth! That's Piia's advice. You have to be tenacious and goal-conscious.

Piia Pantsu

"I guess I have lots of patience. But I'm also very stubborn. I never give up! And the phrase 'It's impossible' – I just don't know those words!"

It really doesn't matter if you ride show jumping or eventing. The basics are the same. To become as good as Piia and the other great stars, you have to learn to do everything correctly, right from the beginning. Everybody was a beginner at some point, no matter how good they became later. That might be good to think about sometimes!

And now you'll get some of the star's best tips to become a good rider. We'll start at the beginning. Here's what Piia has to say:

About your seat
"The most important thing of all, in my opinion, is that you learn to sit in a correct position and train that way! The better you're seated on your pony, the less you'll disturb it, and the better you can help your pony and make it understand what you want."

"How is a horse supposed to jump obstacles faultlessly if it has an unbalanced human on its back?"

So start working on your seat!

"Ride a lot, and ride without stirrups a lot of the time," Piia says.

Make sure you have a good trainer who is very careful – and who'll tell you if you do something the wrong way. That way you can correct small mistakes before they turn into bad habits!

Work on all kinds of seats. When you've worked yourself well and far down in the saddle – from riding without stirrups – you also need to practice standing in a half-forward seat and a forward seat. You have to find your balance, with springy ankles and knees, and follow the horse without falling forward.

You should be able to stand over the horse and still use your leg aids as well.

About equipment:
Equipment is another basic thing. Make sure your saddle is just the right size and lies well on your pony's back. It should rest evenly over the back and not pinch or chafe anywhere.

Make sure the bridle fits well. It mustn't be too high – but on the other hand, it mustn't hang too low, making it jangle in the mouth, so that the horse can put its tongue over the bridle.

The noseband should also be tightened just right and sit at the right height.

And "just right," that's when you can fit two fingers inside the noseband. When an English noseband is placed two fingers below the pony's cheekbone.

"I don't know how many times I've started a practice pass by adjusting all nosebands that were too high or too low or too tight or too loose," Piia laughs.

The pony's leggings should also be adjusted well and just the right size.

They should protect from hits, but the pony must be able to bend its joints without the leggings hindering and chafing.

It's important that all equipment is correctly adjusted – for the horse or pony, but also for yourself.

"It doesn't matter if you ride in boots or in shoes and short chaps, it's important that they're the right size and fit well," Piia says. "It's hard to use leg aids if your boots are too big!"

The helmet also mustn't be too big. It has to sit tightly and firmly on your head – without squeezing or pressing. Gloves are good. And don't forget warm underwear in the winter. Indoor riding rings can be cold as everybody knows.

About practicing:
You need to practice a lot – and you need somebody to help you.

"You have to remember that nobody has gone far in this sport without lots of support and help from people around them," Piia says.

In other words, remember how important your parents and other helpers are!

You need someone who wants to, and can, drive you and go with you, someone to wait, watch, help, pick you up … Both at the riding school, in the beginning, and later for practice sessions and competitions.

This sport will occupy a lot of evenings and weekends, as everybody who has participated in it knows.

It's also important that you get as much out of your training as possible.

"Always make sure that your pony is warmed-up well before you start practicing," Piia says.

Make sure you walk the pony for at least 10 or 15 minutes, and then trot at an easy pace for about 10 more minutes before you begin the actual practice session.

"The horse needs at least 20 minutes of warm-up to be truly ready," Piia says. "Muscles and synovial fluid (a fluid that lubricates the joints) must be warmed up, or the risk of hurting the horse increases a lot."

And then, between each session, work with the tips your trainer has given you.

Your daily workout is what makes you and your horse improve.

About encountering and solving problems:
So, what can you expect from your training? No pony improves all the time. There will always be setbacks, no matter how great your horse is. This is completely normal.

"Little problems actually are a good thing," Piia says. "They make you become a better rider. You get to think, and maybe try something new, and find a way to move on."

If your pony is a little lazy, Piia's tip is that you work a lot with tempo changes. Go quicker and then more slowly. Work with changes from walking to trotting, from trotting to halts, from trotting to galloping.

A horse that is a little slow needs to get faster, in its mind, to make it react faster, and in its body.

A pony that's too hot, on the other hand, needs to slow down; to cool down.

"Work with long, relaxed sessions in an even tempo," Piia suggests.

The main thing is to be methodical. This goes for any horse.

Work out a plan for your riding sessions. Stick to that plan. Follow the same structure (more or less) for every riding session, no matter what you are doing. Warm up. Take a break. Work and practice. Take a break again. Stretch and let the horse relax. Walk.

About preparing for a competition:

Sooner or later it will be time for you to enter your first competition.

"Preparation is half of riding, and that goes for everything!" Piia says.

Talk to your trainer. Plan everything. Prepare everything ahead of time.

And remember:

"Never get brand-new equipment – and then save it, in mint condition, to use for the first time in competition. Make sure you always ride with the equipment you're going to use in the competition. Both you and the horse have to get accustomed to it. You have to know that everything works well – before you go to the competition," Piia says.

And another thing:

"Don't hang any more stuff on your pony than it really needs," Piia says.

"I don't like too much 'bling' and glamor," she says. "You don't have to have lots of brass and clasps that clang and ring. They are more distract-ing than useful!"

The warm-up before a competition should also be methodical. And calm. Remember Piia's motto: "Preparation is half of riding!"

Warm up the same way you would in a regular practice session. Practice tempo changes and maybe a few turns. Make sure that your pony is obedient and attentive. It should listen to you – but still be calm. At that point it's time to ride onto the course. Then do your best, even if you have butterflies in your stomach…

At the first competition you will probably be ner-vous. That's just how it is for most people. Piia still feels a little scared when she remembers her first competition.

She was still a beginner and hadn't done much jumping.

"It was a little club competition at the riding school. The obstacles were 20 inches. I had this little pony, a gray named Tiny. When I got my start signal the pony just took off, at full speed – and I ended up in front of the saddle, on the pony's neck… But I hung on!"

Piia also remembers the best, most wonderful competition she experienced as a beginner:

"I was jumping with one of the ponies at the riding school. Its name was Mistrel. Everything worked out great, we were faultless, and I got my first ribbon!"

Piia and Mistrel came in fifth. In Finland, fifth place means a yellow ribbon.

"I still think that's the most wonderful ribbon I ever got," Piia says.

A PRACTICE TIP FROM PIIA:

Put three poles on the ground on the course or in the indoor ring. Place them on the midline, parallel to the long sides. Then ride a serpentine with three turns. Ride across the poles. Practice riding evenly, and with nice turns and graceful moves. You can practice this routine at a walk or trot.

When you've become experienced enough to gallop, you can practice this routine at a gallop, too. Change gallop every time you "jump" the pole on the midline. The turns, tempo and balance are the most important things to concentrate on. If you want to, you might try putting the poles up as cavalettis and doing the same exercise.

Good luck!

In conclusion

Jumping really is a diverse sport. It bothers me if my students arrive at a jumping lesson and ask how high the fences are going to be. It's not pure height that makes a fence challenging. The horse is the one doing the jumping. The rider's tasks don't change much, not even when the fences get higher. Clearing a fence is merely the culmination of all the other riding that you have to do to get there.

Horses and riders of varying levels can jump. It's important to familiarize yourself will many types of jumping exercises, so that you'll be able to choose the ones most suitable for your skill level. If you've jumped courses of low fences, you can add a higher fence to the end of a gymnastic line – even though you'll not yet be up to jumping an entire course of high fences. And an experienced competition rider can also practice rhythm and control over a couple of low single bars. It's vital that you carefully plan your jumping training. You shouldn't jump solely for the joy of jumping, but also to practice the skills you'll need over a course. You should also remember not to jump everyday. Even a competition rider's training program includes dressage, trail riding, longe-reining, and rest days.

Both horse and rider will need a lot more experience before tackling cross-country fences. Trail riding skill tasks can also be challenging, even though your horse doesn't have to take a single jump. These obstacles highlight the trust between horse and rider. It's not the obstacle that's most important, but the teamwork. Without teamwork, things won't go well in the long run. Training should also be fun! And that goes for both horse and rider. You won't get results if you're grinding your teeth.

I wish you plenty of fun and success over the fences!

Tiina Vainikainen

Notes